TOTALLY
CRUSHED

CANDY APPLE BOOKS...
JUST FOR YOU.
SWEET. FRESH. FUN.
TAKE A BITE!

TOTALLY CRUSHED

by ELIZA WILLARD

candy
apple

SCHOLASTIC INC.

New York Toronto London Auckland Sydney
Mexico City New Delhi Hong Kong Buenos Aires

ISBN-13: 978-0-545-02814-1
ISBN-10: 0-545-02814-0

Copyright © 2008 by Eliza Willard

All rights reserved. Published by Scholastic Inc.,
557 Broadway, New York, NY 10012.
SCHOLASTIC, CANDY APPLE, and associated
logos are trademarks and/or registered
trademarks of Scholastic Inc.

12 11 10 9 8 7 6 5 4 3   8 9 10 11 12/0
Printed in the U.S.A.   40
First printing, January 2008

J
Fic

✿

For N.J.B

TOTALLY CRUSHED

Spirit Week, Day 1

Monday: Valentine's Day

CHAPTER ONE

HEARTS AND FLOWERS

"Pretend you're me, looking at you," Phoebe said over the phone. It was first thing Monday morning and she'd called me for a Spirit Week Outfit Check.

"We really should get videophones if we want to do this right," I said.

"Forget the videophones," Phoebe said. "Now, look at yourself in the mirror. How many hearts do you see?"

What was this — *Sesame Street*? I counted up the number of hearts on my clothes and jewelry. Two heart earrings, plus at least six hearts on my belt, plus dozens on my red-and-white top . . . can't forget my socks . . . yikes. Too many to count.

"Annabel?" Phoebe said. "I don't like that silence. If it takes you this long to count up your hearts, you're wearing too many."

"I thought I was restraining myself," I said. But I knew she was right.

Phoebe King, my best friend, is the practical type. She always goes for comfort over style. Normally, I'm the one prodding her — ever so gently — to kick it up a notch, fashionwise.

But Valentine's Day is my weakness. And this year was a double whammy: Valentine's Day happened to fall on the first day of Spirit Week. The theme for the day was Red and White. We were actually *required* to wear valentine-inspired clothes. The invitation to turn myself into a walking valentine was more than I could resist.

If there's one holiday I'm prepared for, it's Valentine's Day. I love hearts and flowers, and my wardrobe shows it. I have a closet full of red and white, sprinkled with a liberal dash of pink and a touch of sky blue. I've got heart T-shirts, heart sweaters, heart dresses, a heart tote bag, and so much heart jewelry I could open my own store. I'd call it: *I Heart Jewelry*.

"Annabel," Phoebe said. "Take off at least one heart garment now. Remember what Sam told you last year? *Girls* like hearts. *Boys* are scared of them."

"Last year? Phoebe, I told you never to mention last year to me again."

4

"Come on, Annabel," Phoebe said. "You've got to get over the Jude thing. You can't spend the rest of your life refusing to speak about sixth grade."

"I don't see why not."

Sixth grade was torture. I had a major crush on this totally cute boy named Jude Harmon. But he barely knew I existed. So last year on Valentine's Day I decided to make sure he couldn't ignore me any longer. I had a Brilliant Plan.

I decided to send him a valentine. I made it myself — a huge red lace heart covered with smaller hearts. It was as big as Jude's head and much . . . heart-ier.

At first I planned to send the valentine anonymously, but then I realized that might not help me win Jude over. If he didn't know who I was, how would he realize his undiscovered crush on me? So I decided to sign the card. But I wanted it to be perfect, so I practiced my signature about a thousand times before I signed the card. I wrote *Annabel Annabel Annabel* over and over again until my hand hurt. After practicing for hours I had a lovely, grown-up-looking signature, the kind my father uses when he signs a check. A big swooping *A* followed by a long squiggle. An illegible squiggle seemed much more sophisticated than clear-as-day grade-school block printing. And so I signed the beautiful Valentine _____ . It looked *très chic*.

The next day I went to school early and taped the valentine on Jude's locker. Then I went around the corner and waited for him to find it. Phoebe found me hiding there.

"What are you doing?" she asked me.

"Waiting to surprise Jude." I pointed to the huge valentine I'd stuck on his locker.

"Awesome," Phoebe said. "I'll keep you company. He's going to love it."

The two of us crouched around the corner, watching. It seemed to take forever. We got cramps in our thighs and had to sit down.

Jude came into school at last. He opened the valentine, read it, smiled, then looked around. When he turned my way, I instinctively ducked.

"What are you doing?" Phoebe said. "Get out there! Let him find you."

"Okay. Okay! I know — it's silly," I said.

I worked up the nerve to peek at Jude again, but it was already too late. He'd stopped Ari Berg as she passed by on her way to her locker.

"Hey, Ari," he said. "Thanks for the valentine. It's really nice of you."

She paused, glanced at the card, then beamed

at him. "You're so welcome, Jude! I'm glad you like it!"

"I wasn't sure who it was from at first," Jude said. "All I could make out was this big *A* . . . but then I realized the card had to be from you. I mean, what other girl has a name that begins with *A*?"

Annabel, you idiot! I thought. *Annabel!*

Ari laughed. "I have the worst signature! Totally unreadable. Like, learn to write, right? I'm so glad you figured it out! Happy Valentine's Day!"

It was unbelievable. Phoebe pushed me into the hall. "Get out there!" she said. "Don't let Ari take credit for your valentine!"

I stumbled into the hall and cleared my throat loudly. Jude and Ari glanced over at me.

"Hi!" Ari said. "Need a cough drop or something?"

"No, thanks," I said. "I — the valentine —"

Ari reached into her bag and tossed me a cough drop. "Here you go." She turned back to Jude, who was totally ignoring me.

"So, Ari, do you want to do something this weekend?" Jude said. "My older brother's having a party, and he said I could invite a few friends. . . ."

The two of them walked away, chattering about how much fun they were going to have at Jude's brother's party. They ended up going out for the rest of the year. Jude never did learn my name. So much for my Brilliant Plan.

"Next time you give someone a valentine, practice signing your name *clearly*," Phoebe advised. "You know, just in case you want the person to know who the card is from."

"Thanks, I'll remember that," I said.

"Giant hearts are boy repellents," Sam said when I told him the whole story.

"Boy repellents?" I said. "Jude sure liked it."

"He didn't really like the heart," Sam said. "He liked Ari."

Sam and I have been friends since first grade. That's the only reason he gets away with speaking to me so frankly.

"Well, if boys don't like hearts, what do they like?" I asked.

"Comic books," Sam said. "Sci-fi. Pro wrestling. Sports . . ."

"That's not what *boys* like," I said. "That's what *you* like."

Sam shrugged. "Same thing."

"Maybe I should start wearing a pro-wrestling outfit to school," I said. "I could be Annabel the Cannibal. 'She eats boys for breakfast.' How would that go over?"

Sam brightened. "With a face mask?"

"Whatever it takes," I said.

"Most guys would love that." Sam really seemed excited by this idea. Typical.

"I'm sure they would," I said. "But it's not happening."

The rest of sixth grade was torture. Every time I saw Jude, there was Ari. It was a constant reminder of what a chicken I was. And also of the dangers of bad handwriting.

Luckily, Jude's family moved away last summer, and he and Ari broke up. Seventh grade was a chance for a fresh start.

I was determined to have a better Valentine's Day this year. I guess that's why I went overboard with the hearts. Too much enthusiasm.

"I'm taking off my socks," I said into the phone. "That only lowers the heart count by eight."

"Annabel . . ." Phoebe's voice rose, a warning. "Lose the heart-riddled shirt and put on a plain one. Plain white."

"Okay." I knew she was right. "What about you? What are you wearing?"

"You'll see," Phoebe said.

"No fair."

"It's not really describable over the phone."

"Not describable?" What could it possibly be? To wear something indescribable wasn't like Phoebe. She's not the type to go overboard like me. "Now I'm really curious."

"So are you walking to school with Sam?" Phoebe asked.

"That's a weird question," I said. "Of course I'm walking to school with Sam. Like always." Sam and I have either walked or been driven to school together every day since the first grade, unless one of us was sick — and Phoebe knew it. She was clearly trying to steer the conversation away from her mystery outfit. But I didn't mind — I love surprises.

"Good," Phoebe said. "I'll meet you guys on the school steps. And I better not see more than ten hearts on your body. *Ten*, Annabel."

"Okay, okay," I said, tugging off my heart headband. I settled on a red skirt, a white top, a cute sweater with a big heart on the back, my red heart earrings and matching bracelet, and a red barrette to brighten up my hair, which is brown and boring and can use any help it can get.

The Winchester Middle School mascot is a pirate, Winchester Pete, so the overall Spirit Week theme is always pirate related. But this year, for me, the theme was Valentine's Day. *Happy*

Valentine's Day, not *Sad* Valentine's Day. I was going to make up for sixth grade if it killed me.

Finally, confident that my heart count was low enough to keep me from being a walking boy-repellent, I grabbed my backpack and started for the door to meet Sam.

"Wear your coat!" Mom called from the kitchen.

"But Mom, it's Red and White Day!" I don't have a red or white coat. "And it's not that cold out."

"I don't care if it's Go to School Naked Day, you're not leaving this house without a coat."

"But my coat is blue," I said. "It will ruin my look."

She marched out of the kitchen and pulled my coat off the hook by the door. "It's February, for heaven's sake." I put my coat on, and she kissed me good-bye. "Happy Valentine's Day, honey. We'll have a surprise for you when you get home. Dad's making a red velvet cake for dessert tonight."

"Mom, if you tell me what the surprise is, it's not a surprise." That's why I love surprises — *real* surprises — they've been so rare in my life. Mom ruins them every time. I can't remember a single birthday or Christmas where I didn't know exactly what I was getting ahead of time. Somehow, Mom never got the part of a "surprise" where you don't give it away. Basically, she has a big mouth.

"Oops. Sorry, honey. Have a good day! And remember — surprise cake tonight!"

When I got outside, Sam was just crossing his lawn to meet me. He was wearing a white T-shirt with red sweats and red sneakers. His down jacket was dark orange. Close enough.

"Happy Valentine's Day," I said.

"Happy Valentine's Day," he said, punching me on the arm. "Let me guess — you're wearing about fifty hearts under there."

I flapped open my coat to show him he was wrong. "I am not," I said. "I kept the heart count to under a dozen."

"Good job," Sam said. "Thanks to Phoebe, right?"

"Hey, give me a little credit," I said. "Besides, you're dressed up, too."

"I'm only doing it for Spirit Week," Sam said. "Otherwise you wouldn't catch me dead in this much red."

"Even if it was an all-red pro-wresting outfit? For, say, Sam the Sinister?"

"Ha, ha, ha. Seriously, I want our class to win this year. I don't want to get toasted like last year."

"Sixth grade never wins Spirit Week," I said. "They're the youngest. They're new to middle school. They can barely grasp the concept."

"Maybe so," Sam said. "But seventh grade can win. And we're going to show the eighth-graders who's boss."

The rules for Spirit Week are pretty simple. Each class gets points for participation and enthusiasm, costume quality, and creative Pirate Festival booths. We also play games at the Pirate Festival on Thursday and earn points for our grade each time we win. You lose points if members of your class don't dress up for the theme days or compete in the games. The winning grade gets to have a pizza party instead of classes the following Monday afternoon, which makes the whole thing totally worth it. Spirit Week is the funnest week of the school year by far.

"Pizza party here we come," I said. "Hey, we get our carnations today. Did you buy any white ones?"

The week before, the cheerleaders had held a carnation sale to raise money for their new uniforms. The flowers cost a dollar apiece and the cheerleaders deliver them on Valentine's Day by taping them to your locker with a tag on each carnation telling you who it's from. The carnations have a color code: white for teachers, pink for friends, and red for crushes. I ordered white ones for all my teachers, and pink ones for Phoebe and Sam. I didn't buy any red flowers, but that didn't mean I wasn't hoping to get one myself.

Not that I liked anyone special. Hardly. But I thought it would be so cool if somebody liked *me*. Spirit Week ends with a big seventh-grade skating party on Friday — it's the social highlight of the year. Everybody knows what those skating parties are like: holding hands through woolen mittens, sharing mugs of hot chocolate, slipping and sliding on the ice and "accidentally" bumping into your crush . . . I *really* wanted a boy to ask me to the skating party. As a date. It would be my first.

"I bought a white carnation for Mr. Dubrow. He's the only cool teacher," Sam said. "You?"

"I got them for all my teachers. Why ask for trouble?"

Sam laughed. "You're such a kiss-up. Smart move, though."

"What about red carnations?" I asked.

"What about them?" Sam said.

"Did you order any?"

Sam kept his eyes on the sidewalk. He wouldn't look at me. He had a tiny, tight smile on his face and his cheeks got all pink.

"You did!" I said. "Who is it?"

"I'm not saying anything."

"Come on, you can tell me. Did you really send someone a red carnation?"

"Wouldn't you like to know?" he said.

"Who? Who?" I asked.

"Did you see the game last night? I think Duke's going to make the play-offs."

"Don't change the subject!" I said. "But Maryland's going to crush them. Tell me who you got a red carnation for!"

Had Sam really bought a red carnation for a girl? That meant he liked someone — a lot. But who?

I'd never thought of Sam liking somebody that way. We'd been friends for so long, I didn't think of him as a boy that someone could, you know, like or go out with. He was always just Sam to me.

As we walked up the street toward school, I tried to look at him with fresh eyes, tried to imagine him as crush material. Sure, I liked him. But could I ever *like* him? *Can I imagine having a crush on Sam?*

He's tall for seventh grade — and he's got shaggy brown hair that gets in his eyes sometimes. His eyes crinkle in a nice way when he smiles. *Hmm,* I thought. *I guess he is kind of cute.* I hoped the girl he'd ordered a red carnation for would think so, too . . . whoever she was.

"Sam Arkin sent someone a red carnation," I chanted, hoping to tease the answer out of him. It didn't work. He smiled but his lips were sealed.

"I'll find out soon enough," I said, but the suspense was killing me.

CHAPTER TWO

TRUE CONFESSIONS

Phoebe was waiting for us in front of the school as promised, impatiently chomping on blueberry bubble gum.

"Sorry, Annabel. I can't let you into the building." She blocked me with her arm. "Spirit Week dress code violation. The blue coat has to go. No colors other than red and white allowed within fifty feet of Winchester Middle School property." She squinted at Sam's coat. "What color is that — rust?"

Sam looked down at his jacket. "Um, I guess you could call it rust. But it's in the red family."

"I'll let it slide this time," Phoebe said. "But you're on notice, bud."

I laughed. *She* was wearing blue jeans, black sneakers, and a green coat — not a speck of red that I could see. She's tall and has untamable blond curls that she'd bunched into a fat ponytail with a white elastic, but that elastic seemed awfully tiny to qualify for Red and White Day. "Where's *your* valentine outfit?" I asked.

"Ta da." She unzipped her coat. Underneath she wore a red superhero T-shirt with a big white *V* on it. "Victor to the rescue." Phoebe's younger brother, Victor, thinks he's a superhero called Kid Victorious. He's ten. Phoebe's parents tolerate this by letting him dress like a superhero most days. Phoebe thinks he should have grown out of it by now. We're afraid Victor is doomed to be a dweeb for life.

Sam grinned. "Now *that's* the Valentine's Day spirit."

"No, it isn't," I said. "The shirt just happens to be red. And it just happens to have the letter *V* on it. It has nothing to do with Valentine's Day. I'll let *you* slide this time," I teased Phoebe. "But you're on notice, girl."

She laughed.

The first bell rang, so we all went inside. "See you at lunchtime," Sam called, heading left toward his locker. Phoebe and I went the other way. Our lockers are next to each other since my last name (Lawson) comes right after hers (King) on the alphabetical class list. That's how we met last year, on the first day of sixth grade. I showed up on the first day of school and there she was, taping a poster of Spider-Man to the inside of her locker door. (She doesn't like to admit it, but the superhero fixation runs in the family.) She's over her Spider-Man phase now — she *says*. Sometimes I wonder.

We strolled down the eighth-grade hall. "Wow," I said. "Doesn't everything look great?"

The Spirit Week committee had decorated the school with hearts and balloons and red and white streamers. A big poster reminded everyone of the Carnation Code: white for teachers, pink for friends, red for crushes.

"Better than the usual toxic industrial green, that's for sure," Phoebe said.

Two popular eighth-graders, Josie Park and Theo Demopoulos, leaned against a locker, holding hands. In one arm Josie held a big heart-shaped candy box.

"It's their one-year anniversary," Phoebe said. "They started going out on Valentine's Day last year."

"I didn't know that," I said. "Seems like they've been together forever."

"Theo gave Josie a red carnation," Phoebe

said. "Then he asked her to go to the skating party with him. And that was that. They've been together ever since."

"That's so romantic," I said.

"I know," Phoebe said. "Annabel, you're the heart expert. How do you think you know when you *really* like someone?"

I glanced at her, a little surprised. Usually *I* was the one with the gossip about who liked who and how they got together. Though I'd hardly call myself an expert. Phoebe suddenly seemed uncharacteristically interested in Valentine's Day. *And* she wouldn't meet my eye. Now I was suspicious.

"Well," I said. "I think I've got it figured out. When you really like someone, there are signs. The first one is butterflies in your stomach, worse than on a test day. Then you get goose bumps on your forearms. Finally, you get a spacy, head-spinning feeling I call Crush Dizziness."

"Have you ever felt the signs?" Phoebe asked.

"Two out of three," I said. "But since I had a stomach flu at the time, the butterflies might not have been from a crush."

"But how do you know?" Phoebe asked. "You've never had a real boyfriend."

"That's true," I said. "But I've seen a lot of movies, listened to a lot of songs, and read a lot of books."

"Still," she said.

As usual, Phoebe was right. I've liked plenty of boys, but so far none of them had returned the favor. I even had a few so-called "boyfriends" in elementary school — boys who sat with me at lunch or invited me to their birthday parties, only to stop as soon as some other boy started teasing them about being a "cootie-coated girl-toucher," or some other inventive nickname. Then the boys would all run off to poke at a dead frog they found. Like rotting amphibian corpses aren't loaded with cooties. My point being: A boy who dumps you for a dead frog doesn't count as a real boyfriend.

Across the hall, Josie opened her giant box of candy and fed Theo a chocolate. I sighed. To think it all started with a red carnation.

"Wouldn't it be great if something like that happened to *us* this year?" I said. "If we got red carnations, and someone asked us to the skating party?"

"*Really* great," Phoebe said. "If you could get a red carnation from anyone at school, who would it be?"

"Hmm." We started walking again, and turned on to the hall where our lockers were. I glanced at all the kids around me, especially the boys in their red-and-white outfits. I'd already run through the possibilities in my mind, over and over.

"Well, there's Charlie," I said. Charlie Mason and another boy kicked a balloon back and forth. His red T-shirt said PIRATES RULE. His eyes looked even bluer than usual, and that's pretty darn blue. "He's cute. And he broke up with Claire Donnelly over Christmas break."

Phoebe nodded. "That's good."

"And I always liked Oliver Goodrow," I said. Oliver was leaning against his locker, looking dashing in a red blazer and long white scarf. "He's kind of sophisticated. We have Spanish together, and he rolls his *r*'s like a tiger — *rrrrr*."

"Oliver's nice," Phoebe said. "But you do know he's not European."

"I know." Oliver's from Ohio. "But still — look at that scarf. He pulls it off like a Frenchman. Or at least a French Canadian."

"For sure."

Down the hall a blond boy slammed his locker shut, then beat a sophisticated drum rhythm on the outside of it.

"What about Serge?" Phoebe asked. Serge Kutarsky was our class drummer boy.

"He's a little noisy for me," I said. "But if he wants to give me a red carnation, I won't say no."

Charlie, Oliver, and Serge were all perfectly likable guys, but I didn't have crushes on them. Secretly, I was hoping for a surprise. Hoping that someone I'd never noticed, never thought about before, would appear out of nowhere and sweep me off my feet. Or off my skates, if I was lucky enough to go to the skating party with a boy.

"What about you?" I said. "If you could get a red carnation from anyone — who would you choose?"

Phoebe blushed. She made herself busy digging books out of her locker. But I could see her ears, and they were redder than her Kid Victorious T-shirt.

"You like someone," I said.

"No, I don't," she said.

"Yes, you do," I said. "Phoebe, it's so obvious."

She pulled her head out of her locker and finally looked at me. Her face was magenta.

This was big. The weird thing was, I couldn't imagine who in the world she could possibly like. I had absolutely no idea. And we were supposed to be best friends.

"Who?" I said. "Who is it? Phoebs, I'm your best friend. If you can't tell me, who can you tell?"

"In a way you're the worst person in the world to tell," she said.

"Why?" I said.

"Because — you know him."

"Know who? Who are you talking about?"

"All right," she said. "I'll tell you. But you have to promise not to laugh."

"I promise," I said. "Tell me before my head explodes."

"Okay," she said. "I like . . . Sam."

"Sam?!?" At first the name did not compute. *Sam? Sam who?* "You mean, Sam Arkin? My next-door neighbor Sam?"

She nodded. She looked so embarrassed I could tell this was a heavy crush. Like, really serious. Still, I found it hard to believe.

"You like Sam Arkin," I said one more time, for confirmation.

"Yes," she said.

"You," I repeated, pointing right at her so it would be perfectly clear which *you* I was talking about, "like *Sam —*"

"Stop it, Annabel. Yes, me. I like Sam."

"For how long?" I asked. "How long could you keep a secret like this from me?"

"I don't really know," she said. "I just looked at him one day last week and it hit me. I like him."

"That's so great!" I squealed. I was beginning to realize what this meant. My best friend liked my other best friend. Fantastic! My two favorite people

24

in the world — as a couple! What could be better? Or more efficient? Phoebe could have a boyfriend, and Sam could have a girlfriend, and my life wouldn't have to change at all.

"Do you think he likes me, too?" Phoebe asked.

Hmm. I had no idea. But I remembered how evasive he'd been when I asked him if he'd bought anyone a red carnation. He definitely liked *someone*. Why shouldn't that someone be Phoebe?

But I didn't know for sure and I didn't want to get Phoebe's hopes up. I had to be careful.

"He never tells me stuff like that," I said. "But I have a feeling he likes somebody. I'll see what I can find out."

"Thanks, Annabel!" The bell rang. We slammed our lockers shut and headed to class. "You're the best best friend ever."

Yes, I thought, feeling pretty proud of myself. I was ready to help my two best friends find happiness. Even though there was no boy on my own horizon — yet — at least my friends would live happily ever after, thanks to me. I felt like a fairy godmother. *I am the best best friend ever, aren't I?*

Carnation delivery time was only a few hours away. The thought made me shiver with excitement. Would I get a red carnation? Would Phoebe? By lunchtime we'd know!

CHAPTER THREE

THE WRONG BOY

Phoebe's confession — her crush on Sam — made my head spin. I was so stunned I was almost late to Spanish. Señora Gomez shut the door behind me as I slipped into a seat in the front row. Señora Gomez started right in with vocabulary.

Un clavel blanco, she wrote on the board. *A white carnation.*

She was wearing red from head to toe — red shirtdress, red tights, red pumps, red bracelet. No white. Maybe she figured that by lunch she'd have a white carnation to add to her outfit — at least one. She sure had flowers on her mind.

"*Quisiera un clavel blanco, por favor.* Who can translate?"

Oliver Goodrow raised his hand. "I'd like a white

carnation, please." Then he glanced my way and smiled. Did that mean something? Was he thinking about me when he said the word *carnation*?

"Muy bien," Señora Gomez said. *"Quisiera un clavel blanco. Es una indirecta."* I looked up *indirecta* in my glossary. It means "hint."

I was glad I'd sent her a flower — so she'd get at least one. Even the teachers had Carnation Fever. Would lunchtime ever come?

After Spanish, then gym, then the longest math class in academic history (*If x = 1 carnation,* Mr. Mackey, our teacher, said, *and y = no carnations, how do we solve this problem?*), the lunch bell finally rang. I shot out of algebra like a spitball through a straw. Students flooded the halls, laughing and squealing. The lockers looked like floats in the Rose Bowl parade, covered with pink and red flowers. Mostly pink, but there was enough red on display to give a girl hope.

I passed Claire Donnelly's locker, which was covered with carnations. She and her best friend, Jude-stealing Ari Berg, had loads of pink ones and five red ones between the two of them. I wondered if Claire's ex, Charlie, had sent her one. Maybe Jude had phoned one in for Ari from wherever he'd moved to. Everyone thinks Ari and Claire are so nice — everyone except for me and Phoebe. Somehow we seem to be the only ones with the X-ray vision to see through their facades.

"Claire, you got two reds? Go you!" Ari said. Ari is all long, dark lines: long legs, long straight dark hair, catlike dark eyes. Phoebe and I call her the lean, mean, iceBerg machine. We don't claim it makes sense.

"How many did you get?" Claire asked Ari. She's the shorter, rounder, blonder beta girl to Ari's alpha.

"Three," Ari said. "But don't feel bad. Three is only one more than two. Three and two are practically the same."

"I know arithmetic, Ari," Claire said. "I'm aware that three is one more than two."

"Oh, look!" Ari snatched up the tag from one of Claire's carnations. "You got one from Bologna Breath. Isn't that sweet?" Ari sniffed the flower. "It even smells like bologna. I wonder how he did that?"

Bologna Breath's name is Calvin Carter, and his breath does smell like bologna, probably because he eats bologna every day for lunch. Still, as nicknames go, it was pretty harsh.

Claire snatched the carnation back and tossed it into her locker. "Guess he breathed on it. Let's go to lunch."

"If we see Bologna Breath in the cafeteria, you should sit with him, Claire," Ari said. "I won't mind, really."

"That's okay," Claire said.

"No, I mean it. You two would be cute together," Ari said.

"Cut it out, Ari. . . ."

I rounded the corner and dashed to my locker. Phoebe hadn't arrived yet. I saw her locker first — a sea of pink. No red. Rats.

Then I saw mine. *Yes!* I got five pink carnations — and a red one!

This was it! Who could it be from?

My fingers trembled as I pulled the red flower off my locker. The pink ones could wait. A tag was wrapped around the stem. I turned it over.

It said, "From Sam Arkin."

I read it again, just to be sure there was no mistake.

"From Sam Arkin."

That had to be wrong. Better read it again.

"From Sam Arkin."

No. *From Sam Arkin?* No!!!!

"From Sam Arkin."

This couldn't be.

My heart stopped. *Sam? The girl he likes is . . . me?*

Sam plus me. That equation was impossible. To put it mildly. Completely, utterly, totally impossible. So impossible it could only exist in the same bizarre parallel universe where I don't like hearts, Kid Victorious doesn't like superheroes, and chimps on roller skates rule the Earth.

But no, there it was in black and white. "From Sam Arkin." Sam had sent me a red carnation. And red stands for "crush." The Carnation Code had spoken.

Phoebe bounded toward me down the hall, almost flying in her Kid Victorious T-shirt, eager as a puppy to see if she'd gotten any flowers. *Phoebe* . . . What was I going to do? This would break her heart. I couldn't let her know, not yet. I tossed the red carnation into a dark corner of my locker and flashed her my biggest, fakest smile, which made me feel like I was impersonating Ari Berg. Not a good feeling. So much for me being the best friend ever.

"What'd we get? What'd we get?" Phoebe asked as she scanned her locker. Her face fell. "Nothing but pink. Oh, well. Did you get a red one, Annabel?"

I shook my head. "All pink, too." I tore a pink flower off and read the tag. It was from Phoebe. "Hey! Thanks, Phoebs."

She waved the pink carnation I'd sent her. "Thanks to you, too. And look — here's one from Sam." Sam had sent her a pink carnation. Because they were friends. Just friends.

I could tell Phoebe was a little disappointed, but she's a good sport and she tried to hide it. One of her down-to-earth qualities is the ability to accept reality without too much whining. My mother mentions how much she admires that quality every time we have liver for dinner. Liver is disgusting and I'm not afraid to express my feelings about it by whining. Phoebe would just smile and choke it down.

"It was nice of Sam to send me a pink carnation," Phoebe said. "At least he remembered me."

"That's right. Of course he remembered you," I said.

"Maybe that means something," Phoebe said. "You know how boys are. He might be too shy to send a red flower."

"He might be," I said. But I knew better. Sam wasn't shy. And he wasn't afraid of red carnations. The proof was hiding in the back of my locker.

"We've got four days until the skating party," Phoebe said. "Sam could still ask me to go with him."

She's an optimist. I've always liked that about her. But in this case her optimism was painful for me to take.

I didn't know what to say.

"It's possible, right?" Phoebe said. "Don't you think?"

"Sure," I said. "Anything's possible."

Especially when you live in a parallel universe ruled by roller-skating chimps.

The crowd in the hall began to thin as people headed for lunch. Sam rounded the corner and made a beeline for us, a big smile on his face. Oh, no!

He was expecting a big happy smile from me, no doubt. A thrilled thank you, and maybe even a hug. Gack!

The hug was not happening. Not with Phoebe standing right there. Or under any other circumstances.

Phoebe saw him and lit up. Sam was sure to say something about the flowers — and Phoebe would be heartbroken. I couldn't let that happen. I needed some time to straighten out this mess.

"Hey!" Sam said. "How did you —"

"Lunchtime!" I said. "Gotta go!" I grabbed Phoebe's arm and dragged her away toward the cafeteria before Sam had a chance to finish his Sentence of Doom.

"Annabel! What are you doing?" Phoebe tried to free herself from my kung-fu grip, but I wasn't letting go. I could tell she was annoyed with me. I didn't care. "Why didn't you give me a chance to talk to Sam? He might have asked me to the skating party!"

"Sorry," I said. "I'm just so hungry! I'm dying for some —" We'd reached the cafeteria. The menu was posted on the door. I scanned it in search of inspiration. "Brussels sprouts! Yes, Brussels sprouts. Gotta have some."

We were safely inside the cafeteria door. I let her go. She rubbed her wrist and glared at me. "Brussels sprouts?" she said. "Since when — ?"

"Great source of vitamin C," I said, dragging her to the food line and hoping I was somewhat right.

"If it's vitamin C you want, a glass of orange juice will take care of it," Phoebe said, tugging her arm away.

I barely listened. I had bigger problems. Like finding a way to keep from breaking the hearts of my two best friends.

CHAPTER FOUR

GOOD CHEMISTRY, BAD CHEMISTRY

Lunch was not good. For one thing, I had to choke down a plate of Brussels sprouts, and it turns out I like them about as much as I like liver.

I led Phoebe to a table in the back of the cafeteria, far from where we usually sit (smack in the middle), hoping that Sam wouldn't see us. We ended up at a half-empty table with Calvin "Bologna Breath" Carter, who was eating a bologna sandwich, and Darryl "Ick" Eckstein at one end, and this guy named Alex Hoffman at the other. Unlike everyone else in school, Alex was not wearing red and white. Not a speck of red or a speck of white. Even Calvin and Darryl were wearing dorky red Christmas sweaters. Darryl's had a reindeer on the front and Calvin's had a snowman.

Alex was wearing blue jeans and a black turtle-neck. No sense of valentine spirit at all.

He was sitting alone, listening to his iPod while he ate, and kind of nodding his head along to the music. He wore his earbuds a lot and kept to himself. I didn't know him very well.

"Why are we sitting way over here in Siberia?" Phoebe asked. "Hey — there's Sam! Let's go sit with him."

Sam had found a place with some of his guy friends — Jon and Chris and a bunch of other boys — at a front table, where they were laughing loudly and throwing grapes at each other. Sam can get rowdy when he's with the guys.

"We can't go over there," I said. "We'll end up with smushed grapes in our hair."

Darryl Ick gave one of his trademark snort-laughs. Phoebe and I glanced in his direction. He had peanut butter and jelly stuck in his braces.

"It can't be any worse than this table," Phoebe muttered. "I'll take grapes in my hair over Darryl's see-food any day."

"I'd go in a second," I lied. "But Sam's table is too crowded. We'll see him later. We see him all the time! What's the big deal?"

"I guess," Phoebe said, averting her eyes from another snort-laugh.

I turned my head the other way, toward Alex. He was still bopping his head to the music, oblivious to Darryl's braces and Sam's food fight. Off in his own world.

"He's got the right idea," Phoebe said.

"He's kind of cute," I said, admiring his straight black hair that was just a little too long and sparkly greenish eyes. "What's his story?" Alex is in science with me and Phoebe and in my Spanish class. His accent isn't very good, but that was really all I knew about him.

Phoebe shrugged. "He's new this year. Maybe he plays in a band? I thought I saw him carrying a guitar case once."

"That's cool," I said.

"I guess," Phoebe said. "If you like the standoffish type."

I'm a school spirit girl, rah rah, heart on my sleeve (and on every other item of clothing) kind of person. So no, I don't like the standoffish type.

At Sam's table, they had moved on from throwing grapes to throwing bread balls. "I'm not crazy about the food-fight type, I know that," I said to Phoebe.

Phoebe gazed longingly across the room at Sam's back. *Smack!* Jon got him right in the forehead with piece of pineapple from his fruit cup. "Food fighting doesn't bother me. Come on — let's go over there. I want to shoot peas across the table at Sam." She stood and picked up her tray, ready to move.

Wow — they were really made for each other. If only Sam knew it. "Phoebe, can we please stay here? I — um —" I tried to come up with a good excuse. "My stomach hurts."

"But you just wolfed down that plate of Brussels sprouts," Phoebe said.

"Yeah," I said. "That's why my stomach hurts."

She gave me one of her penetrating, X-ray-vision stares, like she could see right through me. "Brussels sprouts? Your stomach hurts? Something doesn't add up here."

"No, no," I said. "Everything adds up. One plus one equals two. Everything adds up perfectly."

She didn't say anything else about it, but she squinted at me suspiciously for the rest of the lunch period. Uh-oh. She was on to me. It's hard to pull anything over on Phoebe. When she's on to you, the best thing to do is just stay away.

"I've got to go," I said. I quickly gathered up my stuff and hurried out of the cafeteria to my next class. I was early, so I sat alone in the empty classroom and doodled hearts in my notebook.

I tried to avoid Sam for the rest of the day, but it wasn't easy. He's in my World Events class. I usually sit with him, but that day I hid in the corner next to Charlie Mason instead. Sam kept trying to catch my eye, but I refused to look at him. Charlie grinned at me, same as always. I wondered if he'd bought anyone a red carnation.

When the bell rang I rushed out of class before Sam had a chance to catch me.

Finally, last period, Phoebe and I had Physical Science with Ms. Winkler — and, more importantly, without Sam. I'd made it through the day. Only the rest of my life to go.

"Put the carnations away, people," Ms. Winkler said. Her own desk was piled with white flowers. "Let's get down to work. We're continuing with our chemistry unit."

Somebody tossed a pink carnation across the room.

"It's been an exciting day, but I need you to calm down now," Ms. Winkler said. "Please pair up and work on the review problems at the end of Chapter Seven."

Oh, no. Pair up. Phoebe and I always pair up

together. And normally that would be great. But right now being around her made me nervous because she wanted to talk about Sam and the carnations. It was the romantic stuff I usually loved to talk about. But all of a sudden I didn't feel like talking about romantic stuff. I had a Terrible Secret. And I knew that Phoebe, who has excellent lie-dar, might find my silence suspicious. I had already pushed the boundaries of believability at lunch.

Besides, I have to concentrate when it comes to chemistry. And although it does come naturally to Phoebe, which would make her a good partner under happier circumstances, today being near her would only be a distraction.

Phoebe glanced across the lab table at me, ready to say, "Pair up?" But, thankfully, before she had a chance, Tessa Jones tapped her and said, "Be my partner?"

I smiled at Phoebe to let her know it was okay with me. She shrugged and said "Sure," to Tessa.

Phew. Dodged that one.

But now I needed a partner. I looked to my left. There sat Alex Hoffman, spinning around on his lab stool in his not-red-and-white clothes.

"Do you have a partner?" I asked him.

He abruptly stopped spinning and said, "No."

"Want to be my partner?" I said.

"Okay."

I looked over the review problems. They were about how carbon dioxide bubbles form when metal carbonates interact with an acid. Yawn.

"So how come you're not dressed for Red and White Day?" I asked Alex, just to make conversation. Well, that and I was curious, too. "Did you forget that it's Spirit Week?"

"No, I didn't forget," Alex said.

I waited for him to say more, but he didn't.

"Oh," I said.

We read a little more about acids and bases, but I couldn't concentrate. Technically, Alex had answered one of my questions. But he hadn't answered the other one. His answer didn't explain why he wasn't dressed in red and white.

I tried again.

"So, if you didn't forget about Spirit Week, why aren't you dressed for Red and White Day?" I asked. "Our class will lose points because of you, you know."

Alex shrugged. "I didn't feel like wearing red and white today. I'm not sure I have any red clothes, anyway."

"That's impossible," I said. "Everybody has something red, somewhere in the back of their closet." I couldn't imagine a human who owned no red clothes.

"Maybe I do," Alex said. "I didn't look."

"But it's Valentine's Day." I couldn't help pressing him. "Everybody's supposed to dress up for it."

"Why?" Alex looked kind of baffled.

"Because," I said. Why didn't he get it? "It's fun."

He shrugged again. "Even when I try to go along with the rules . . . somehow everything I do comes out different. So usually I don't really try."

"I have no idea what you're talking about," I said.

"Like, if we're all supposed to wear white, I put on a shirt I *think* is white, but it turns out to be beige," Alex said. "Or my voice gets loud the second everyone else gets quiet. . . . It's hard to explain. It's like I have social dyslexia."

"I get things wrong all the time, too," I said, thinking of my closet full of heart-covered clothes that Phoebe and Sam will never let me wear. "I keep thinking next time I'll get it right."

"I guess I just gave up trying to be like everyone else," Alex said. "What does wearing certain colors have to do with school spirit, anyway? Aren't your activities and what you contribute to the school more important?"

"Well, sure, but . . ." His point was hard to argue with. That didn't make it right. "You can contribute to the school *and* do Spirit Week," I said.

"Yeah," he said. "You can do lots of things."

Hmm. He was a strange one. But then, when I thought about it, what boy wasn't?

I thought of the red carnation lying in the back of my locker. Instead of giving it to Phoebe, who liked him, which would have led to a happy ending for everybody, Sam gave the flower to me, who didn't like him (*that* way), and it only led to a lot of trouble. Why couldn't he like the girl who liked him? Was he *trying* to stir up trouble? Why, why, why?

"What is created when you add an acid to a base?" Alex said. He was actually working on the chemistry review problems. I had more pressing issues on my mind.

"I think the answer is salt," Alex said. "What do you think?"

"You're a boy, right?" I was going to get to the bottom of this.

He blinked at me. "Um, last time I checked. I'm just going to write 'salt' down here, unless you have an objection."

"Salt. Yeah, salt," I said. "Can I ask you a

question? Since you're a boy, you must be an expert on them. Right?"

"I never thought about it," Alex said. "I'm more of an expert on rock guitarists of the early 90s."

"Interesting," I said. "Let me just ask you a question and you answer from a boy's point of view."

"Okay."

"Why do boys always have to be different?"

"Different? What do you mean?" Alex glanced around the lab at the other boys. "Far as I can tell, they're all wearing red and white. They're not being different at all."

"I don't mean their clothes," I said. How could I explain it without giving away my Terrible Secret? I didn't want Phoebe to overhear our conversation and guess about Sam.

"I mean," I said very quietly, "like, if a girl likes a guy, why does he always have to like a different girl, a girl who *doesn't* like him, instead of the girl who *does* like him?"

Alex blinked. "Does this have anything to do with chemistry?"

"Yes," I said. "In a way, it does."

He blinked again. "Is the answer 'salt'?"

He was not getting me. "Let me rephrase the question," I said, pulling my stool a little closer to his. "Here it is: Why do boys have to make things so difficult? With girls, I mean."

"Boys?" he said. "They're not the ones who make things difficult. Girls are impossible. I can't even understand what they're saying half the time."

Touché.

"Girls get things wrong, too, you know," Alex said. "They misread our signals and twist the meaning of things we say. Sometimes a guy says something to a girl and he thinks he's being clear as day but she totally gets the wrong idea, anyway."

"That's exactly what I mean," I said. "It's like we're speaking two different languages."

Across the room, Claire twirled two carnations, one red and one pink, between her fingers. *Pink means friendship, red means a crush*, I thought. *It's so simple.*

"If only we had a code," I said. "A perfectly clear signal, so a girl would know exactly what a guy means. And the other way around. Like the Flower Code."

Alex laughed. "The Flower Code! That's pretty simple all right. Just three choices: teacher, friend, or crush, and nothing in between."

"Too simple?" I asked.

"Yeah," Alex said. "What if you want to say something like, 'I might like you if I got to know you better, but then again, I might not'? How do you say that in carnation language?"

"I don't know," I said. "A pink-and-red hybrid flower?"

"You can't," Alex said. "People are more complicated than that. Except maybe teachers."

"I wish they didn't have to be," I said.

"Welcome to the real world," Alex said. "Hey, at least it keeps things interesting."

I looked over at Phoebe. This was interesting, all right. But I'd rather be bored than see my best friend totally crushed.

Spirit Week, Day 2

Tuesday: Pajama Day

CHAPTER FIVE

FROM BAD TO WORSE

I lay awake all night, staring at the ceiling and worrying about Sam and Phoebe.

I didn't want to break Sam's heart. I didn't want to lose his friendship. But what could I possibly say to him that wouldn't hurt his feelings? I lay in the dark, tossing and turning, rehearsing different scenarios in my head.

"Sam, I'm so flattered that you like me, but you've got peas on your shirt from your last food fight and so, you understand, I just don't see you as boyfriend material."

Too blunt. Next.

"Sam, I really like you, but don't you think you and Phoebe have more in common? You like pro-wrestling, she used to like superheroes (and I suspect she secretly still does), and really, is there a difference between the two? They're all men in colorful tights."

Too off-topic.

"Sam, I really like you — but so does Phoebe. And she's my best friend. So I'm going to step aside and let the two of you find happiness together. My heart is broken, but it's a sacrifice I'm willing to make."

Too melodramatic.

"I wish I could go out with you, Sam, but I have a policy: I don't date neighbors. Weird, I know, but you know what they say. . . ."

What *did* "they" say, anyway? Something about good fences making bad dates?

Not believable. And too confusing.

Nothing seemed right. I couldn't see any way to let Sam down gently and keep him as a friend. And I really, really didn't want to lose his friendship. But I didn't want to lose Phoebe's friendship, either. And I didn't want to be Sam's girlfriend . . . or even his crush.

I had no choice but to avoid Sam for as long as I could — or until I got a brilliant idea. Maybe time would take care of everything for me. Time heals all wounds, et cetera. Maybe Sam's crush was only temporary and would disappear in a few days. Stranger things have happened.

What if the whole red carnation thing was nothing but a joke? What if I was getting myself all worked up over nothing?

Ha ha, Sam. Very funny.

That was also possible. And it would be great. We'd all laugh, and everything would go back to normal.

But something told me this wasn't a joke.

My best hope was that the whole thing would blow over if I just stayed away from Sam for a few days. Then he'd forget all about his silly soul-searing crush on me! I'm not easy to forget, I know. The Annabel tattoo doesn't wash off so easily. But it would be for the best.

Help, I thought. *I'm losing it.* I'm a basket case without sleep.

At 6:30 A.M. I gave up trying to sleep and got out of bed. I wanted to have plenty of time to slip out of the house before Sam got there. Step One of my Avoid Sam at All Costs Plan was: Never walk to school with him again.

Getting dressed should have been easy. It was Pajama Day and I was already wearing pajamas. You'd think all I'd have to do was put on some slippers and go.

But nothing in a girl's life is that simple. I wasn't about to wear the pajamas I'd been tossing and turning in all night to school. They were wrinkled, not to mention hideous: bulky blue flannel covered, for some reason, with tiny white schnauzers. I wasn't *that* sleep-deprived.

I opened my dresser drawer and took out a super-cute new pair of pajamas I'd gotten for Christmas. (Mom "surprised" me with them after I cut a picture of them out of a catalog and left it on her dresser. *Es una indirecta. Hint, hint.* They were pink-and-white striped cotton knit and fit perfectly. The kind of pajamas you could almost wear as clothes, or at least work out in.

I brushed my hair and divided it in two cute pigtails tied with red ribbons. For slippers I had the corduroy kind with a good rubber sole, so my feet wouldn't get wet or dirty. And I still had plenty of time to sneak off to school before Sam realized I was gone.

My parents were just getting up as I slipped into my coat. "Off so soon?" Dad said. "Isn't it a little early?"

"I've got a few things to do before school today," I lied. "For Spirit Week. So if Sam stops by looking for me, let him know, okay?"

"Okay, honey," Mom said. She kissed me goodbye. "Oh — guess who's coming over for dinner tonight?"

"It's a surprise," Dad said.

"Yes — Aunt Jenny's coming over to surprise you," Mom said. "She has a little late valentine gift for you. Isn't that nice? I won't give anything away. Let's just say it's heart-shaped, and gold, and hangs from a chain, and you can put tiny pictures inside."

"Um . . . is it a locket?" I asked.

"How did you guess?" Mom said. Dad rolled his eyes.

"I'll try to gasp convincingly," I said. "See you later."

The streets were weirdly quiet at that early hour. The heavy front door of the school squealed as I opened it. My slippers squeaked on the shiny floors and echoed through the empty halls. It was kind of creepy being at school so early.

I looked up to read the chart with the Spirit Week scores in the main hall. Each day of the week was a column at the top and there was a row labeled for each class along the left side of the chart. Monday's score had been filled in: Sixth grade had forty points, seventh grade had sixty, and eighth grade had seventy-five. Great. We were already lagging behind. But the week was young. We could still catch up.

I thought of Alex and his refusal to wear red and white. How many points had that cost us?

I went to my locker, pulled out a notebook, and sat down on the floor to catch up on my Spanish vocab. The halls slowly began to fill up. The girls all wore their cutest pj's, but the boys looked like they'd just rolled out of bed. Most of them hadn't even combed their hair. Phoebe appeared in a very practical pair of dark blue cotton pajamas with red piping around the collar and a thick terrycloth bathrobe for a coat.

"Happy Pajama Day," she said. "Have you had a chance to talk to Sam yet?"

"Talk to Sam?" I said. "About what?"

She squatted down to my level so she wouldn't have to say it too loudly. "You know, about who he likes."

"Oh, right. No, I haven't seen him yet. But I'll find out about it, I promise," I said.

"He said he likes someone, right?" she said.

"Well, he didn't *say* that," I said.

"I wonder if he sent anyone a red carnation," she said, making my heart race nervously.

"Probably not," I said. "I mean, who would he give one to if not you?"

"I hope you're right," she said. "Oh — here he comes!"

I looked up and Sam was speed-walking toward

us. He definitely looked like he had something he wanted to get off his chest.

Sorry, Sammy boy, but that was just not going to happen. I jumped to my feet, grabbed my books, and slammed my locker shut. The first bell rang. Thank you, thank you, thank you, first bell!

"Hi, Phoebe," Sam said. "Hi, Annabel. I —"

"Sorry, I've got a Spanish quiz," I said very quickly. "Can't be late talk later bye!"

I ran down the hall, balancing my books in my arms. I was in such a rush I didn't watch where I was going. *Oof!* I crashed into someone and all my books tumbled to the floor.

"Annabel, are you okay?" Oliver Goodrow's black eyes drilled into mine. He was wearing plain blue pajamas with his initials monogrammed on them. Rumpled yet classic. I felt a little dizzy.

"I'm sorry," I said. "I wasn't watching where I was going."

"No, it's my fault," he said. He knelt to gather my books. "Let me help you with these."

I bent down to pick them up, too. "Thanks so much," I said.

"No worries." He smiled at me.

Señora Gomez stood at the classroom door, ready to close it. "Any decade now," she said, uncharacteristically not *en español*. Maybe the white carnations had softened her up.

Oliver handed me my books and we went inside. *"Hola, muchachos,"* Señora Gomez said. *"Gracias a todos por los claveles blancos."*

"De nada, Señora Gomez," we all said back to her.

"We'll be working on dialogues today," Señora Gomez said. "So everyone pick a dialogue partner."

Oliver turned to me. "Be my partner?" he said.

"Sí," I said. He had a very nice way of peeking out at you from behind his bangs. I could like him, I thought. I really could. Why couldn't Oliver have given me a red carnation, instead of Sam? My life would have been so much simpler. Oliver and I could double-date with Sam and Phoebe. The four of us could go to the skating party together, and go to the movies, and sit together at lunch. . . .

"Ready, Annabel?" Oliver said. Oh right, the dialogue.

Oliver played Paco and I played Maria. All around us, other students were reading the dialogue out loud. Someone with a bad Spanish accent was booming out both Paco's and Maria's lines from the back row.

I looked back. The loud voice was Alex's. He was

reading the dialogue alone. He had no dialogue partner, since Kara was absent that day, leaving the class with an odd number of students. And, of course, he was not wearing pajamas. He was wearing a faded red Nirvana T-shirt and jeans. A *red* T-shirt. *So he does own something red! How annoying. Why couldn't he have worn that shirt yesterday?*

Oliver read the last line with an expert r-r-roll of his *r-r-r's*. Then he glanced back at Alex, too.

"What's with that guy?" he said.

"Social dyslexia?" I said.

"You're telling me."

When Spanish was over, Oliver gave me a little wave and said, "See you at lunch?"

"Sure, see you," I said. Maybe Oliver would ask me to the skating party, even though he hadn't sent me a carnation. That would work. Then, even if Sam asked me, I wouldn't be able to go with him, because I'd already have a date.

Why don't you ask Phoebe? I would suggest to Sam, ever so subtly.

Yes, Phoebe, Sam would say, a lightbulb popping up over his head. *Why didn't I think of her before? I've had a crush on her all this time and I didn't even know it!*

Problem solved.

I stepped into the hallway. Uh-oh. Sam was

headed my way — the real Sam, not the happy fantasy Sam who liked Phoebe. He knew I had Spanish first period and he was definitely looking for me. He was as relentless as a shark, like a heat-seeking missile, or an Annabel-seeking missile, always pointed toward me. I zipped off to algebra as fast as I could.

After algebra, there he was again. And after art class he was waiting for me by the door. I managed to dodge him by pretending I didn't see him, then pretending I couldn't hear him when he called out my name. He chased after me so I used my trump card, ducking into the girls' bathroom. *Ha. Try to follow me in* here, *Sam Arkin,* I thought.

But Sam is clever, and he finally found a way to reach me whether I wanted to be reached or not.

I stopped by my locker at lunchtime and found an envelope taped to the outside.

I opened the envelope. Inside was a handmade card, a collage of cutout photos from magazines. Close up I saw the photos were mostly shards of pictures of bands on stage.

At the bottom was scribbled: "You rock. Your S.A."

S.A.? Sam Arkin?

My heart sank. Sam would not give up. His crush on me was even worse than I thought.

Clearly Sam had a fatal case of Annabelitis. And a few days of ignoring him probably wouldn't be enough to cure it. Not if he was this far gone.

I may not know much about boys, but I know this: They don't put any effort into things they don't care about. So if they *do* make an effort — like cutting out dozens of pictures from magazines and pasting them onto a sheet of construction paper . . . well, that has to mean something.

All I could do was keep avoiding Sam until I thought of a way out of this. But then there was Phoebe. What about Phoebe?

I couldn't just avoid her — she'd know something was up right away. And she'd be hurt. She'd think I didn't like her anymore. I didn't want her to think that, since it was totally not true. And besides, if I avoided Sam *and* Phoebe I'd have no one to hang out with.

I had no choice. I had to tell Phoebe about Sam's crush on me. How could I keep such a gigantic secret from my best friend? If the tables were turned and Phoebe knew that someone I liked liked her, I'd want her to tell me. I would want to know the truth so I could vacuum that boy from my brain as soon as possible.

Besides, the sooner Phoebe knew the truth, the less it would hurt. I hoped.

CHAPTER SIX

WOULD YOU STILL BE MY FRIEND IF I STOLE YOUR CRUSH?

"That outfit's not good enough," Phoebe said. "Or should I say, not *bad* enough. I'd still be your friend if you wore that."

I tossed the plaid Bermuda shorts back in the pile. Phoebe and I were in my room looking for the perfect outfit for Wednesday's Spirit Week theme: Would You Still Be My Friend If I Dressed Like This? I needed Phoebe's advice. Since Phoebe was my best friend, I figured she'd be an expert on what kind of outfit was so heinous it could end our friendship.

I also had an ulterior motive, of course — to tell her about Sam, the red carnation, and his note. Better to give bad news at home than at school, I figured. More private. No witnesses in case of tears, tantrums, or catfights. Still, I kept my head buried in piles of ugly clothes to hide my nervousness.

"You'd really be friends with a girl who wore this?" I held up one of her rejects, a SpongeBob SquarePants T-shirt with a big grape jelly stain on the front. "You're too forgiving." And I secretly hoped she was.

"No, I'm not," Phoebe said. "I just don't take friendship lightly. To lose my friendship, you'd have to do something pretty terrible."

"Like what?" I said.

"I don't know," she said, chomping on her blueberry bubble gum. "I guess like, break a promise, or tell one of my secrets. Or maybe steal a boy from me behind my back. But I know you, Annabel. You'd never betray me that way."

Gulp. Time to change the subject.

"You know what you need?" I dragged some shiny blue fabric out of my bottom drawer. "Electric blue Lycra tights!"

"Ick!" Phoebe held the pants up to her legs. They'd fit her. "Why do you have these?"

"I borrowed them from Mom one year for Halloween," I said. "I was an alien."

"These are definitely alien." Phoebe tried them on. They made her legs flash like strobe lights. "But what did your mom use them for?"

"Aerobics," I said. "The early eighties. Mom loves her fads."

"P.U. I hope this fad never comes back." She checked herself out in the mirror. She didn't actually look bad. Tacky, but not bad. "But what do I wear on top?"

"Hmm. I think we need to go to the source. Mom's room."

"Will she mind?"

"Hardly."

I led Phoebs into Mom and Dad's room and opened the bigger of the two closets. "Behold," I said. "Shoulder pads, neon colors, acid wash jeans, parachute pants . . . and animal print as far as the eye can see, from shoes to headbands. This is where the eighties came to die." I pushed a spotted headband over Phoebe's thick blond hair and left it perched across her forehead. I laughed. "Now *that's* tacky."

"Let me see." She looked at herself in the mirror and burst into giggles. Then she grabbed a zebra-striped bolero jacket. "That's what I'll do — clashing animal prints from head to toe," she said. "Everybody will hate it!"

Once we'd outfitted Phoebe in animal-print splendor, we went back to my room to work on me. I'd settled on a hideous puce T-shirt with a cartoon of a pudgy toddler holding his arms out and saying, "I WUV YOU THIS MUCH."

"That is so gross," Phoebe said.

Paired with baggy gym shorts, X-ray specs, and a bike helmet decorated with aluminum foil bug antennae, I was ready to alienate the entire school.

"What shoes should I wear?" I asked. "Keds?"

"Keds are not nearly repulsive enough," Phoebe said. "If you're going to sink low, you've got to dive all the way to the bottom." She crawled into my closet and came out with the ultimate humiliation, a pair of blue-and-silver moon boots. "What about these?"

"Genius," I said.

"*Why* are these in your closet?" Phoebe asked.

I knew there was no defense, but I gave it a shot. "Well, they're really warm." I tried on the boots. They were a little tight, but I thought I could stand them for a day.

"If they're so warm it's too bad you can't wear them skating Friday." Phoebe said and laughed. "Can you believe the skating party is almost here?"

"Oh, yeah. Friday," I said. "Can't wait." I sat down on my bed. The aluminum foil antennae bounced with every shake of my head. I felt ridiculous. But the time had come to be a real friend and tell Phoebe the truth. "I have something to tell you."

Phoebe's face lit up, and I felt even worse. "Is it about Sam?"

"Yes," I said. "It's about Sam." I took a deep breath. As Phoebe herself had said, I might as well dive all the way to the bottom. "Yesterday . . . I got a red carnation."

"What? Annabel, that's great!" She popped her gum in celebration. "When? From who? Why didn't you tell me?"

"Um . . ." Ouch, this was so hard. "I didn't tell you . . . because of who it was from."

She stopped chomping on her gum. Her face flickered with different emotions, from curiosity to confusion to hurt.

"Wait . . . *Sam*?" The hurt expression was the one that stuck.

I nodded. "I got something else from him today." I showed her the card.

"Wow," Phoebe said, studying the collage. "He really likes you." She swallowed. I felt so bad. If I were in her place, I'd be breaking into tears. Totally overreacting. But she held it together. "So, are you going to go with him to the skating party?"

"The thing is, Phoebs, I don't like him," I said. "Not like that. I swear it's true."

Phoebe let out a deep sigh.

"I believe you." But she wouldn't look at me.

"I don't know what to do," I said. "How can I let him know I just want to be friends without . . . losing his friendship? I don't want to hurt his feelings."

"I don't know," she said. "That's a tough one." She took off her leopard-print headband and played with it.

"I wish he'd like you instead," I said. "My two best friends, together as a couple! It would be so cool."

"Yeah," Phoebe said.

"I can make it happen, Phoebs," I said. "There's got to be a way. I just don't know what it is yet."

She nodded and twirled the headband around her wrist.

"You're not mad at me, are you?" I said. "I promise I never did anything to encourage him. Ever since I got the carnation all I've done is run away from him."

"I'm not mad at you, Annabel," she said. "Not at all." But she was definitely upset. "It's not your fault. I'm glad you told me the truth. That proves you're a real friend."

"And *that* proves that *you're* a real friend." I threw my arms around her and hugged her like the

I-Wuv-You toddler on my ugly T-shirt. "Thank you for not holding this against me. We'll find a way to work it out. I know we will."

"We'll see," Phoebe said. She hugged me back, but not enthusiastically. And she pulled away first. "You can't force people to like you. And by the way," she added, scanning my outfit from antennae to moon boots, "if you dressed like that I would so totally *not* be your friend."

I thought I heard a little bite in her voice — but I laughed it off. "Same here, Tarzan. Tomorrow we'll be the geekiest kids at school. That top alone has got to be worth, like, eight hundred Spirit Week points."

"Yeah," Phoebe said. "Here we are worried about a silly boy, when bigger things are at stake."

"Dressing like this is a sacrifice we'll have to make," I said. "To bad taste: for the honor of the Seventh Grade. Pizza party, here we come!"

"Here we come," Phoebe echoed, but I could tell her heart wasn't in it.

Spirit Week, Day 3

Wednesday: Would You Still Be My Friend if i Dressed Like This? Day

CHAPTER SEVEN

HOW TO REPEL A BOY

"I'll drive you to school today, honey," Mom said.

This was good news. I wasn't about to walk to school in the sleet wearing moon boots, gym shorts, X-ray specs, and aluminum foil antennae.

It's what Mom said next — as inevitable as bad breath following garlic bread — that upset me.

"I'll call Sam's mother and let her know we'll pick him up."

We always drive Sam to school when it's too rainy to walk. Of course we do — we're good neighbors.

So what could I do? Refuse to sit in the car with him? Insist that he trudge to school in the freezing rain wearing an outfit (I didn't know exactly what yet) so ugly it would cause his friends to run screaming in the other direction? The idea was tempting. But how could I explain to Mom why we couldn't pick up Sam? She'd never go along with that.

I would have to ride in the same car as the red-carnation-sending Sam Arkin. But that didn't mean I'd let him talk. I couldn't risk having him bring up the card or the flower — or worse, ask me to the skating party. *Let him try,* I thought. No neighbor of mine was going to be asking me to any skating party. If Sam wanted to take someone ice-skating, it had better be Phoebe.

I borrowed Mom's silver metallic raincoat for extra hideousness and followed her to the car. I slid into the front passenger seat, but Mom said, "Sit in the back, Annabel. It's safer on a slippery day like today."

I knew better than to try to argue safety with Mom. Part One of my plan to avoid Sam, foiled. But I'm not so easily defeated.

I sat in the back, right behind Mom, and buckled up. We drove the twenty yards from our driveway to Sam's. He came out in a *Star Trek* uniform with a furry Wookie head on top.

"Hi," Sam said as he climbed into the car and took in my antennae and X-ray specs. "You're looking dorky." He said it in an admiring way, of course. How else would a boy who's totally gaga talk to the girl of his dreams?

"You should see her without the raincoat," Mom said.

Sam laughed. I made it my business to see that that laugh was the last sound he'd make during that car ride.

I kept as far away from him as the seat belt allowed and practically glued myself to the door. I locked the reflection of my mom's eyes in the rearview mirror in my site and let 'er rip.

"Mom, you know how I've always liked Valentine's Day? Well guess what? I've changed my mind. Yup, that's right — I don't like Valentine's Day anymore. It's — how can I put this? — silly. A just plain silly excuse for a holiday."

"Okay, Annabel," Mom said. "I —"

"No, Mom," I said. "Don't try to talk me out of it. I'm serious. I mean, what was I thinking? Hearts? Sappy cards? Chocolates are great, of course, but who needs a holiday to eat chocolate, know what I'm saying?

"You know what I think the problem is?" I said. "I've grown out of it. I've grown out of Valentine's Day."

I didn't mean a word of that, of course.

"Honey —" Mom said.

I was trying to send Sam a message. Out of the corner of my eye — I was afraid to look at him directly — I could see him shifting uncomfortably in his seat. Every so often he opened his mouth as if he wanted to say something. Sorry, bud. Not gonna happen.

"Valentines are okay if you're a sixth-grader," I said, keeping the patter flowing. "But by seventh grade I really think they're over —"

"Annabel, what are you talking about?" Mom said.

"Valentines, Mom. Don't you think by now I'm way too mature . . ."

Cars were lined up in front of the school building, and the parking lot was a zoo. Parents zipped in and out of the line, cutting one another off, and kids were getting out and crossing in front of the cars. Mom's forehead creased the way it does when she's trying to concentrate. "Annabel, stop talking for a minute, please, before I run over one of these kids."

What was I going to do, keep yammering and be responsible for the death of one of my schoolmates?

So, reluctantly, I stopped talking. And Sam seized his chance.

"Annabel, I really need to talk to you," he said.

"Sorry, gotta go!" I undid my seat belt, opened the car door, and tumbled into the parking lot before Mom had even pulled up to the curb.

I heard her shout, "Annabel! What's wrong with you?" But I didn't stop to apologize or explain. I just bounded in my moon boots through the crowds of kids and into the school building. I pretended I was weightless, running on the moon, each step taking me three feet into the air. No one wearing mere shoes could ever catch me. Then I hid in the girls' bathroom. I would just have to stay there until right before the first period bell.

Ari and Claire came into the bathroom, gossiping and giggling. They somehow managed to look dorky and cool at the same time. Ari wore her hair in Pippi Longstocking braids that stuck out from the sides of her head, with striped socks and a baby doll dress. Claire was dressed in head-to-toe Hello Kitty, topped with fuzzy pink cat ears. They both looked unfairly adorable.

They laughed when they saw me. "Look at you!" Claire said. "I so totally wouldn't be your friend. Where did you even *get* that T-shirt?"

"Great outfit, Annabel!" Ari said. "I wouldn't be your friend, either."

"Just kidding." Claire said. They looked at each

other and cracked up. I was so not in the mood for these two.

"Well, I love your outfits, too," I said. "I wouldn't be your friend, either!"

"Ha ha ha ha!" We all cracked up. Too bad it wasn't really funny. I wished Phoebe was there.

"So what did you say to Serge?" Claire said to Ari, dipping right back into whatever conversation they were having on their way to the bathroom. Then Claire explained to me: "Serge asked Ari to the skating party."

"Cool," I said. "Are you going with him?" I was hoping she'd said yes to Serge so all the other boys hovering around her would have to look elsewhere for dates — like in my direction, for instance.

"I told him I'd think about it," Ari said. She stood in front of the mirror and fussed with one of her Pippi braids. "I'd rather go to the skating party with Serge than with nobody. But I'd rather go with Oliver than with Serge."

Uh-oh. *My* Oliver? Spanish Oliver? Oliver, who I'd hoped might save me from Sam? If Ari was after him I didn't stand a chance. Not much of one, anyway. At least Charlie Mason was still a possibility.

The bell rang and they left. I took a deep breath. This was one stressful Spirit Week.

I waited a few more seconds, then dashed to my locker right before class. My locker door was blissfully note-free. Ahh. Maybe my plan was working: act like a jerk and Sam would stop liking me. It was painful, but for his own good.

I hurried to my first class, breathing a little more easily now. All I had to do was stay away from Sam and, if I had to see him, act totally snotty. Soon Sam would get the message that I am not girlfriend material. Not for him, anyway. And I wouldn't actually have to say the words "I don't like you that way." He'd get over me and fall into Phoebe's waiting arms. Sam and Phoebe would become the happiest couple in human history, and the three of us could be friends again.

That was the plan. I just hoped it would work.

I dodged Sam all day. His Wookie head was easy to spot in a crowd. Just before chemistry, when I thought it was safe, I paused in the main hall to check out the Winchester Pirates' Spirit Week score chart. I found Phoebe there in her animal-print 80s outfit.

"How're we doing?" I asked.

"See for yourself." Phoebe waved her hand at the scoreboard. The eighth-graders were still ahead by ten points, with ninety to our eighty. The sixth-graders lagged way behind with 55.

"That's too bad," I said. "But we can still catch up if everyone participates."

"What do you mean?" Phoebe said. "Everyone is trying their best."

"Not *everyone*," I said. "Alex didn't wear pajamas yesterday."

"Some of the eighth graders didn't wear pajamas, either," Phoebe said. But there was something strange in her tone — she didn't sound as friendly as usual.

"And he didn't wear red on Monday. How many points do you think that costs us?"

"I don't know," Phoebe said. She added a shrug that said, *And I don't care.* Which wasn't like her at all. If she didn't find this topic interesting, I wasn't going to force her to talk about it.

We crossed the hall to the science lab.

"I hope you all read the homework last night," Ms. Winkler said. She was wearing a plastic mustache-nose-and-glasses combo and a blue Marge Simpson beehive wig. "Please pair up to review the questions at the end of Chapter Eight."

I wanted to be Phoebe's partner again. But when I asked her, she glanced around as if hoping to find someone better. Everyone already seemed to be paired off.

"Okay," she said.

"Phoebe," I said. "Are you sure you're not mad about Sam?"

"I'm not mad," Phoebe said. "I told you that."

"I know," I said. "But you're acting kind of weird."

"I'm sorry you think I'm weird."

"I don't think *you're* weird," I said. This was so frustrating. How could she be mad at me for something that was totally not my fault?

I tried changing the subject. "Did you hear Serge asked Ari to the skating party?"

"Did she say yes?" Phoebe asked.

"She's not sure yet," I said. "She's weighing all her options."

"You'll tell me if Sam asks you, right?" Phoebe said.

"I will," I said. "But I'm doing my best to freeze him out. By Friday I'll have been so cold to him he won't want to look at me."

Phoebe opened her science book. "Maybe we should get to work on these review problems."

Speaking of cold . . . *brrr.* I had to warm things up between me and Phoebe or soon I *really* wouldn't have any friends left.

"Phoebe," I said. "Want to work on our pirate costumes together? Maybe I could come over after school."

"Not tonight," Phoebe said. "I've got a ton of homework."

"Homework?" She'd never turned down a chance to hang out just because she had a little homework. "Phoebe, please. It's me, Annabel. I know this isn't about homework." This was serious. I couldn't lose my best friend over a boy. I just couldn't.

"Phoebe, I'm coming to your house tonight whether you want me to or not."

"Fine," Phoebe said.

"I'll do whatever it takes," I said. "No red carnation is going to come between me and my best friend."

She smiled at that, and popped her blueberry gum. A good sign.

CHAPTER EIGHT

KID VICTORIOUS

"Away, Evildoer! I, Kid Victorious, will vanquish you and your villainous kind!"

That night I rang Phoebe's doorbell and this is what answered: a short kid in a red T-shirt with a giant white *V* on it, red footie pajama bottoms, and swim goggles. His blond hair was moussed into a ridge on top of his head. What that ridge had to do with being a superhero, I didn't know. But it certainly helped him look different from your average human.

"*You* go away, Kid Victorious," I said, pushing Phoebe's brother Victor aside. "I'm here to see Phoebe."

Victor blocked my path. "Halt! No pirates allowed in the Fortress of Fortitude."

I rolled my eyes, but I'd forgotten I was dressed almost as weirdly as Victor was. I had on a tricorner hat and a puffy-sleeved white shirt with black pants, boots, eye patch, beard, and a long jacket with gold buttons. I'd brought some other possible pirate accessories in a duffel bag.

"Yo ho ho, Kid Victorious," I said. "For the next three hours the Fortress of Fortitude is going to be Pirate Central. Get used to it."

"Okay," Victor said in a more normal, less super-hero voice. He sure backed down easily. "Phoebe's in her room. Want a snack? We've got stuff in the kitchen."

"If you've got something salty, bring it on," I said, heading upstairs to Phoebe's room. The house smelled good, like cake. Phoebe had set the mood by hanging a skull-and-crossbones flag over her bedroom door. She was just buttoning a pair of knee breeches over white socks and a T-shirt with a skull on it when I walked in.

"What smells so good?" I said.

"I made cupcakes for the Pirate Festival tomorrow," Phoebe said. "To give away at one of the seventh-grade booths. Once they cool we can frost them and decorate them with tiny pirate hats."

"Great! How do I look, matey?" I said, presenting myself for inspection.

"Better than last year," she said. "But generic. We'll need a few special touches to win those extra points."

"Don't worry," I said. "This isn't my whole costume. I brought some other stuff." I rattled the duffel bag over my shoulder.

Pirate Day is big — the highlight of Spirit Week. Everyone dresses up as a pirate and morning classes are canceled for the Pirate Festival. Last year, as a clueless sixth grader, I had a sad little pirate costume — basically an eye patch and a fake beard and that was about it.

But this year I was determined to help the seventh grade win. There could be no slacking in the pirate costume department. I opened my duffel bag and pulled out a stuffed parrot and a little tin chest.

"What's that lunch box for?" Phoebe asked.

"It's not a lunch box," I said. "It's a chest of gold. See?" I opened the chest to show her the chocolate "gold doubloons" inside.

"Ooh," Phoebe said. "That's good."

"I thought we could pass out gold coins to everyone," I said. "Including the judges." Mr. Dubrow, the art teacher, and Ms. Tabor, the gym teacher, were in charge of judging how many points each class earned — and I happened to know they were both chocolate fiends. "A little bribery never hurts, right?"

"Right," Phoebe said. "And what are you going to do with that parrot?"

"I need to find a way to attach him to my shoulder," I said. "So he'll go where I go all day tomorrow."

"I think I've got something —" Phoebe rummaged through a drawer and pulled out a needle and thread. "What if we sew him to the shoulder of your jacket?"

"Um — it's not my jacket," I said. "It's my mother's."

"From what I've seen of her wardrobe, she'd love to walk around wearing a parrot," Phoebe said. "Anyway, we can always pull out the stitches later."

"Okay." If Mom killed me, she killed me, but I was pulling out all the stops.

"Da-da-da!" Kid Victorious burst into the room with a bag of chips. He held a corn chip to his mouth and pretended it was a bugle. "Forward to victory!"

"What are you talking about?" I said.

"He never makes sense," Phoebe said. "He just speaks his own weird superhero language." She took the bag of chips from him and said, "Thanks, K.V. Your services won't be needed any longer."

"Not so fast," Victor said. "Kid Victorious's pirate protection services *will* be needed. And they'll cost you five cupcakes."

"You can have *one*," Phoebe said.

"Three," Victor said.

"*One*," Phoebe said.

"Now get lost or we'll make you walk the plank," I threw in for good measure.

"Walking the plank doesn't scare a superhero who can fly," Victor said.

"Yeah, right," Phoebe said.

Victor stood in the doorway and saluted us. "Underneath his Little League uniform, mild mannered fourth-grader Victor King becomes KID VICTORIOUS! Protector of the meek, vanquisher of evil, unsung hero of the neighborhood! With the help of a magic energy cupcake he gains SUPER STRENGTH to do the near-impossible — keeping Mom out of his sister Phoebe's ugly hair! Will Phoebe appreciate his help? Will she notice if he eats five cupcakes instead of one? Tune in next time for another exciting episode of KID VICTORIOUS! Up, up, and out of here!" He ran from the room with his arms out like wings.

"Don't you mean up, up, and away?" I called after him.

There was a patter of feet in the hall and then

Victor stuck his little pointy head back through the door. "No, I don't." And then he was gone again.

"Don't correct his superhero style," Phoebe said. "It bugs him.

"And I'll definitely notice if you eat more than one cupcake!" she yelled after Victor.

"Show me the rest of your costume," I said.

Phoebe buttoned a white shirt over her tee, put on a gold-trimmed coat, and tied a skull-and-crossbones scarf over her curly hair. "I'm going to be Mary Read. She was a real girl in the 1700s who pretended to be a boy so she could be a pirate." She took a step back to compare our two costumes. "Though how you can tell the difference between a girl dressed up as a pirate and a girl dressed as a boy dressed as a pirate, I don't know."

"It's all in the attitude, I guess," I said. *"Squawk! Aye, matey! All in the attitude!"* I shook my parrot at her to make it look as if he were talking.

"What's your parrot's name?" Phoebe asked.

"Winona," I said.

"Winona the parrot?" Phoebe scrunched her nose.

I shrugged. "I like the name Winona."

Victor jumped into the room, flexing his biceps.

84

"Danger! Danger! The Mothership has penetrated the Fortress of Fortitude and is coming this way!"

"Get out of here, Victor," Phoebe snapped.

Mrs. King stepped into view in Phoebe's door. "Yah!" Victor threw himself against her as if trying to knock her down.

"Sorry, Vic," Mrs. King said. "I don't tumble that easily."

Victor ran into the room and started bouncing on the bed and singing. "Up in the air, up in the sky! VICTORIOUS! Kid VICTORIOUS! Better than you, better than pie! VICTORIOUS! Kid VICTORIOUS!"

"What's he singing?" I asked.

"It's his theme song," Phoebe said. "He made it up. Can't you tell?"

"Catchy." I grabbed Victor by the ankles, mid-bounce, and he tumbled onto the bed. "Hey, I found Kid Victorious's kryptonite — his ankles!"

"Yah!" Victor pounced on top of me.

"Victor, don't attack the guests," Mrs. King said. "Phoebe, I found some old candy corn left over from last Halloween. Do you want to use it on your cupcakes?"

"They're pirate cupcakes, not Halloween cupcakes," Phoebe said. "Besides, that candy corn is from October. It has to be stale by now."

"I was just trying to help," Mrs. King said.

"Victor, I thought you were going to keep the Mothership out of my hair," Phoebe said.

"Yah!" Victor pounced on his mother, driving her from the room.

"Ow, Victor, you stepped on my toes," Mrs. King said. They disappeared down the hall.

"You have a weird family," I said to Phoebe.

"Uh, duh," Phoebe said. She reached into my pirate chest and took a chocolate coin. "So, did you see Sam after school at all?"

"No," I said. Actually, I had seen him through our kitchen window, playing with another neighbor's dog in his backyard. I ducked so he couldn't see me and avoided windows for the rest of the afternoon. "But I have a fabulous new plan."

Phoebe looked skeptical. "What is it this time? Move to Antarctica?"

"No, though I do have the right boots," I said. I looked for a smile from Phoebe but got nothing. Oh, well. "I'm going to get another boy to like me. Tomorrow."

"Tomorrow? How? Are those *magic* doubloons?"

"No. But I have a few prospects. Charlie Mason. Oliver Goodrow. Once Sam sees me flirting with someone else, he'll forget all about me."

Phoebe scrunched her nose. "Um, how are you going to pull that off?"

"I'll switch to offense," I said. "I'll become a super-flirt. Those boys won't know what hit them. If I throw myself in their path they'll be fighting for a chance to ice-skate with me. Isn't that how Ari does it?"

"Yeah," Phoebe said. "And she's really good at it."

"What are you saying?" I said. "That I'm *not* good at getting boys? That I can't get one to like me?"

"Well —" The corners of her mouth dragged down.

Right away I wished I could take those words back. Because getting a boy to like me wasn't the problem. The problem was, the only boy who'd ever liked me — or at least the only boy who liked me now — was Sam.

"I know it's not a great plan," I said. "But I'm desperate! I don't even need a real boyfriend. All I need is to get a boy to ask me to the skating party. That way, even if Sam asks me, I can't go with him. Which frees him up to ask you."

"Annabel," Phoebe said. "I don't want your left-overs. I want Sam to like me for me. I don't want him to ask me to the party just because he can't have you."

"Phoebe, Sam *does* like you," I said. "He just

doesn't know it yet. Once he realizes I'm the wrong girl for him, it will all be clear."

Phoebe sat down on her bed. "Can we talk about something else?" She looked so sad, and that made *me* sad. I realized I'd gotten way too caught up in all this skating party craziness.

"You know what?" I said. "In the end, it doesn't matter who goes to the party with who. The important thing is that we're friends forever."

For the first time in two days, Phoebe looked me in the eye and smiled. That smile was such a relief, like the sun coming out after a rainstorm.

Spirit Week, Day 4

Thursday: Pirate Day

CHAPTER NINE

STOP THE SCURVY

"Breakfast doubloon?" I offered Phoebe a chocolate coin.

"Thanks." She took one and ate it. "Nothing better than chocolate in the morning, right after you brush your teeth."

"Aaarrr," I said to indicate agreement.

Thursday dawned nice and sunny, so I managed once again to sneak out of the house and walk to school before Sam had a chance to catch me. I met Phoebe at our lockers and we hit the Festival in our fabulous pirate costumes. So far, the perfect Pirate Day.

The Spirit Week committee had turned the gym into a giant pirate ship, with black and red crepe paper, skull-and-crossbone flags, and a cardboard bow and stern at either end. The walls were lined with booths for snacks and games where you could win "pirate booty" or, if you lost, "walk the plank." The "plank" was a balance beam with a big air mattress underneath.

The gym was packed with pirates growling, "Yaarr! Yaarr!" Phoebe left her cupcakes at our class's snack stand. Then she and I strolled from booth to booth, eating Hard Tack with Maggots (scones studded with chocolate chips) and drinking jugs of "rum" (apple juice) marked with a skull and crossbones.

"What does a dyslexic pirate say?" Phoebe said.

"I don't know," I said. "What?"

"Rrraaa!"

We laughed. Mr. Dubrow and Ms. Tabor were casing the gym with clipboards, smiling at everyone and making notes. I stopped and opened my treasure chest for them.

"Doubloon?" I offered.

Mr. Dubrow took one. "Thank you, Annabel."

Ms. Tabor took one, too. "How clever. I love chocolate!"

"You do? I had no idea!" As I've mentioned, acting surprised is my specialty.

"I'll take another one," Phoebe said, helping herself.

"Delicious," Mr. Dubrow said. "Nice parrot, too."

"Remember — we're in grade seven!" I said as they walked away scribbling on their clipboards. "That should score us a few points," I said to Phoebe.

She tapped my arm. "There he is."

Sam was ambling across the gym. He was dressed as Captain Hook, with a real hook jutting out of one sleeve, which he waved at us.

"Uh-oh," I said. "Hide!" Phoebe and I scooted away to another booth. "Time to put my plan into action."

"Just don't take too long," Phoebe said. "We can't avoid Sam forever."

I kept an eye on Sam all morning, staying just out of his reach. Avoiding him kind of put a damper on things. I love Spirit Week, but I couldn't enjoy it so much this year. I was just so worried about bumping into Sam. Even worse, I was beginning to miss him. If only he wasn't the cause of my problem, he would have been a great person to talk to about it. Phoebe gives good down-to-earth advice, but Sam is great for crazy, off-the-wall ideas that actually work. Plus, he's just fun. Walking to school without him was a little lonely.

"Remember last year?" Phoebe sighed. "That song we wrote? 'I Love You Just the Way You *Arrrr*'?"

Last year's Pirate Day, Sam and Phoebe and I

ran a Sea Chanty booth, a kind of pirate karaoke. We all sang sea chanties (most of which we made up) and got everyone else to sing along, even the teachers. We gave out booty for the most enthusiastic singer, best pirate accent, and funniest pirate dance. Sam and Phoebe and I had spent the whole weekend before at my house writing the sea chanties and printing them out to pass around.

Our Sea Chanty booth was so popular that this year Ari and Claire signed up to run it before any of us had a chance. Phoebe and I stopped to watch Ari croak out a lame rendition of "Shake Your Booty" while shaking a box of gold coins like a tambourine. Please.

"Yeah," I said. "But 'Hook Me Matey One More Time' was a classic."

"We're a good team, the three of us."

"Yeah," I said. *Too bad Sam had to ruin it by getting a crush on me,* I thought.

"*Hola,* Annabel." Oliver looked amazing in a red silk cape with a jewel-handled plastic sword at his side. He even had a fake curly mustache. "What's the lunch box for?"

"It's not a lunch box," I said. "It's a treasure chest." People had been mistaking my treasure chest for a lunch box all morning. I opened it up. "Would you like a gold doubloon?"

"Is it worth anything?" Oliver asked.

"It's chocolate, you dork," Phoebe said.

I elbowed her. Oliver was one of my prime skating party candidates and I didn't want to spook him.

Phoebe quickly backpedaled. "Uh, I mean, it's chocolate, uh, *foodpork*. That's what the pirates called candy in the olden days. Chocolate foodpork."

Oliver gave her a funny look. "Chocolate foodpork? That doesn't sound very good."

I pressed a coin into his hand. "It's tasty, I promise. It's just chocolate. Really."

"Uh, okay. Thanks." Oliver backed away toward the Sea Chanty booth.

"Sorry," Phoebe said. "I'll try to keep my mouth shut while you work your magic."

I looked over at Oliver. He was watching as Ari and Claire jumped up and down, screaming the lyrics to some song I couldn't recognize.

"What song is that?" I said.

"How could anyone possibly tell?" Phoebe said.

Even though their singing was bad, they were making so much noise they began to attract a crowd to their booth.

Suddenly, Oliver tapped me on the shoulder. I hadn't even noticed him come back. "Hey, Annabel — can I have some more foodpork?"

"What? Oh, yeah." I opened my treasure chest and gave him two more coins. "There you go."

"Thanks."

Oliver drifted away.

"Did you see that?" I said to Phoebe. "Oliver came back for more doubloons — even though he thinks they're called chocolate foodpork. Do you think that means anything?"

Phoebe shrugged. "It either means he likes you, or he likes chocolate."

"Or both," I said. "He could like me *and* chocolate."

"Totally possible."

"Annabel! Phoebe! Over here!" Charlie Mason waved us over from the Pirate Face Painting booth. He was all done up with fake gold teeth, scars, a mustache, and a temporary tattoo of a mermaid.

"Aha," I said to Phoebe. "Let's go say hello to my future skating partner."

Phoebe gave me a warning look. "Remember, Annabel. Don't go overboard."

"I won't," I said. "Trust me." I opened my pirate chest as we approached the booth. "Hi, Charlie," I said. "Chocolate foodpork?" Drat that Phoebe. Now that weird word was stuck in my head. "I mean, gold doubloon?"

"Thanks." He took a couple of chocolate coins. "Nice parrot."

"I call her Winona."

"Winona?" Charlie said. "How about 'Polly'? Or, I know — 'Zandora.' It sounds Goth."

"I like Winona," I said.

"So, you need any pirate supplies?" Charlie said. "I think you do. You look too clean to be a pirate. How about some tooth black? Makes you look like you've been out at sea for months. Aye, and ye haven't seen a toothbrush in many a morning."

"Shiver me timbers." Phoebe wiggled her eyebrows at me. I laughed.

I dipped my finger in the tooth black. "Does it taste bad?"

"No," Charlie said. "But it doesn't taste that good, either."

"What else have you got?" I asked.

"Scars," Charlie said. "That's what you need. To make you look scary. A scar, maybe two."

"Okay," I said. "Scar me."

I leaned down and he pasted a rubber scar across my forehead. I checked myself out in the hand mirror. "Yikes. One more."

He handed me another rubber scar. I stuck it under my eye.

"Now you look like you've survived a duel or two," Charlie said.

"Thanks," I said. I smiled at Charlie. He smiled back. His eyes caught mine and stayed locked on me for a good three seconds. I counted it out — one Mississippi, two Mississippi, three Mississippi . . .

Phoebe tapped my hand. "Sam alert," she whispered. "Headed this way, two o'clock."

Shoot. I had to get out of there. I forgot all about my plan for Sam to see me flirting and dashed behind the booths to the bleachers, where pirates could sit and eat their snacks. It was crowded back there, and we were somewhat hidden.

"Did you notice how long Charlie stared at me?" I said. "Three whole seconds! And he kept piling scars on me like he didn't want me to leave."

"I guess so," Phoebe said.

"I think he was about to ask me to the skating party," I said. "If only our Sam-sighting hadn't interrupted him."

"We can go back to his booth in a few minutes and give him another chance," Phoebe said.

We started up the bleachers to find a seat. "Annabel! Hey, Annabel! Wait!"

I turned around. Oliver was running toward us. Oliver was out of breath when he caught up with us — a sure sign, I thought, of skating-party passion. But then he said, "Do you have any more of that foodpork left?"

"Oh. Sure." I gave him two more coins.

"Leave some for the rest of the school," Phoebe said. I elbowed her again, more halfheartedly this time.

"Thanks!" Oliver went back to watch the Sea Chanty Karaoke disaster.

"I think it's the chocolate he likes," I said. "Not me."

"The evidence is pointing that way," Phoebe said.

I brightened. "Unless he's using the chocolate as an excuse to talk to me —"

Phoebe shook her head. "Give it up, Annabel."

Phoebe and I climbed up a few more rows and sat down in front of the one person in the entire school who was not wearing pirate clothes: Alex, of course. He was wearing black jeans and a black turtleneck.

"Hey," Phoebe said. "How come you're not dressed as a pirate?"

"I am dressed as a pirate," Alex said. "I'm an intellectual pirate. I steal copyrighted property."

"What?" Phoebe and I both stared at him.

"It's a big problem," he said. "People copy

movies and music and software and sell them without paying the people who created them."

"And that's called intellectual piracy?" I asked.

He nodded. "It's a serious issue, and I feel someone should draw attention to it." He plucked his black turtleneck. "This is my 'intellectual' costume."

Phoebe blinked. "Are you sure you didn't just forget it was Pirate Day?"

"If he did you'll never get him to admit it," I said.

"She's right," Alex said.

"Come on, kids." Ms. Winkler waved from the gym floor at the three of us. "We're playing Stop the Scurvy and we need more players."

"Let's go," I said. "The seventh grade needs points." Phoebe and I started down the bleachers. Alex stayed seated. I went back to get him. Our class couldn't afford for him to keep sitting out. "You, too, Einstein."

I pulled him toward the growing circle in the middle of the gym. On the way we passed Mr. Dubrow and his clipboard. "He's an intellectual pirate," I said, pointing at Alex. "Did you get that? Clever, right? I think it deserves extra points for originality."

"I'll make a note of it," Mr. Dubrow said.

Alex, Phoebe, and I joined the lumpy circle.

Music played, and Ms. Winkler started the game by giving Calvin Carter an orange. Calvin tucked the orange under his chin and turned to the girl next to him, who had to take it from him with *her* chin without using her hands.

"Thank goodness we're not next to Bologna Breath," Phoebe whispered to me.

"Yeah," I whispered back. "Or Darryl Ickstein."

The orange passed slowly down the line from chin to chin until one eighth-grade guy couldn't quite get a grip on it and it dropped to the floor. That guy was out.

"Yes," I said. "Eighth grade loses a point."

The girl next to him picked up the orange and started again.

The orange moved closer and closer to me. A girl passed it to Alex. Alex passed it to Phoebe. Phoebe passed it to me. I turned to pass the orange to the person next to me . . . and found myself face-to-face with Sam. Had he been standing next to me the whole time?

"Yo ho ho," Sam said, leaning in to take the orange. His face was so close I could smell the cinnamon gum he was chewing.

"Oh!" I was so startled I lifted my chin and the orange fell to the floor with a dull thud. I didn't think, I just acted. I pulled myself out of line and cried, "I'm out!" The last thing I needed was to go chin-to-chin with Sam. My cheeks burned as I realized that my hasty getaway had probably cost my grade an all-important spirit point.

I tried to run out of the gym, but the Stop the Scurvy game snaked across the whole basketball court. Pirates kept getting in my way. It felt like a bad dream — I couldn't break through the circle and get out!

I glanced back and caught a look passing between Sam and Phoebe. It said, *Is this the usual Annabel nuttiness or has she just dug a crawlspace under her all-time low?*

Good, I thought. Maybe they'd bond over my weird behavior. Maybe it would draw them together.

I finally got to the gym doors and burst through them, running down the hall and not stopping until I reached my locker. I stopped to catch my breath and then opened it. An envelope fluttered to the floor. On the outside was my name written in black marker and decorated with skulls and crossbones.

Please don't let it be from Sam, I thought.

I opened it. It was another collage. This time the card said "Yo ho ho! I'm hooked on you!" Sam had just said those very words to me. The card was signed, again, "S.A."

I laughed, and I melted a little in spite of myself. It was sweet. I had to admit it felt good that a boy was sending me secret notes and stuff like this. . . .

But then I felt sad. Poor Sam! If only I wanted Sam to be the one. If only I could think about him that way.

But I couldn't. I just couldn't. And even if I could, I wouldn't. Phoebe was crazy about him, so it would still be a problem. I'd have to choose between my best girl friend and my best guy friend. And I couldn't do that.

Why couldn't I have both best friends? Why couldn't things go back to the way they were before?

I folded up the note and put it away. I guess my plan to repel Sam with coldness wasn't working at all. It seemed to be backfiring. And I still hadn't found a skating party date to block him with.

I sank to the floor. The halls were quiet, completely empty. Everyone was at the Pirate Festival, having a wonderful time. Everyone except for me. I was stuck out here, hiding from my second-best friend.

How did I get into such a terrible mess? I wondered. And how would I ever get out of it?

CHAPTER TEN

ANTI-LIKE POTION

"What happened to you?" Phoebe whispered.
"Where have you been?"

"Nurse's office," I said. "Stomachache."

It was true. I'd planned to fake a stomachache, but by the time I saw the nurse I didn't need to. I was so worried about Sam and Phoebe that my stomach really did hurt. I took off my pirate hat, jacket, and parrot, and lay on a cot to rest.

After a few hours I thought it was safe to go to science lab. It's my last class on Thursdays, and Sam's not in it. And I knew Phoebe would be worried about me if I didn't show up.

So I slipped into lab, two minutes late. Ms. Winkler asked me if I was feeling all right. I told her I was much better.

"We're studying the properties of carbon

dioxide gas," Ms. Winkler said. "Why don't you partner with Phoebe?"

"Great." I grabbed a stool next to Phoebe, across the lab table from Alex, who seemed to be working alone. He raised an eyebrow at me in greeting.

"Step one," Ms. Winkler said. "Pour a small amount of vinegar in your petri dish."

Phoebe poured some vinegar in our dish. "That was quite a meltdown," she said quietly.

"I know," I said. "I saw Sam standing there with his goofy smile, waiting to take the orange from me, and I freaked. I didn't know what to do. I was afraid if I went neck-to-neck with him he'd get the wrong idea. Did he say anything after I left?"

"Not really," Phoebe said. "He didn't have time. I ran after you but I couldn't find you anywhere. I didn't think of checking the nurse's office." She paused. "Sam must feel like he has the plague, the way you freak at the sight of him."

"I don't want to make him feel bad," I said. "I really don't. But I don't know what to do." I thought of the note I'd just gotten and considered telling Phoebe about it. But I decided not to. She already knew things were bad. No need to make her feel worse.

"Step two," Ms. Winkler said. *Oh, right —*

science lab. "Add one teaspoon of baking soda to the vinegar. Watch what happens."

I measured out a teaspoon of baking soda and stirred it into the vinegar. The mixture bubbled and fizzed.

"Why don't you stop washing your hair?" Alex said.

"What?" Was he talking to me? He was looking right at me. Stop washing my hair? What kind of thing was that to say?

"If you want to make a guy stop liking you," Alex said. "That might work. Or you could try wearing a garlic necklace. That keeps vampires away."

Phoebe laughed. "If you wear a garlic necklace you'll keep *everybody* away."

"Or ouyay ouldcay ytray alkingtay otay imhay inay Igpay Atinlay," Alex said.

"What?" I said.

"Pig Latin," he said. "If you only talk to him in Pig Latin, he might get annoyed and not want to speak to you anymore."

"That's an idea," Phoebe said.

"I don't want to make him not speak to me," I said. "I want to make him stop *liking* me — *that* way. But I want to keep him as a friend."

"If only we could make an anti-like potion,"

Phoebe said. "One sip and he'd be cured! No more crush on Annabel."

"Yeah," I said. I picked up the plastic soda bottle Phoebe had put on the floor. She'd already drunk about half the root beer in it. I unscrewed the cap and poured a little vinegar into the bottle.

"You're done with this, right?" I asked her.

"Um, I am now," she said.

I shook the vinegar/root beer mixture. It fizzed mildly. "Needs eye of newt," Phoebe said. "But since we're out of eye of newt, baking soda will have to do." She dumped a few spoonfuls into the bottle. "Now to mix it together —"

She capped the bottle and shook it. The liquid foamed up inside, a hideous pale brown. "Hey," I said. "It really looks like an anti-like potion. It could turn anyone off anything."

"Let's test it out on someone." Phoebe gave the bottle one more shake, then unscrewed the cap. *Spurt!* The sticky brownish liquid shot out of the bottle, spraying everyone around us with anti-like potion. Alex buckled over laughing.

An instant later, Ms. Winkler was glowering at the mess we'd made. "What happened over here?" she said. I froze. Uh-oh. Now we were going to get it.

She held up the bottle, studying the liquid left inside. "A perfect example of what happens when you create too much carbon dioxide in a closed container — kaboom! Luckily, this combination of chemicals isn't dangerous." She smirked at us.

Phew.

"But it's still messy," Ms. Winkler said. "You two will have to stay after class to clean this up."

"Yes, Ms. Winkler," Phoebe said.

"We're sorry," I said. It would have been worth it if the anti-like potion really worked. Not that I actually believed in it . . . but now we'd never get a chance to find out.

Alex was still laughing.

"Sorry we got anti-like potion on you, Alex," I said.

He touched his wet hair, then he started wrapping it around his finger and making messy waves. "That's okay. It makes a good styling gel. A little sticky, but great hold." He patted his hair flat and made long bangs. We all cracked up.

After class, I mopped the floor while Phoebe wiped down the counter. "Seriously, Annabel," she said. "You have to talk to Sam. You can't avoid him any longer."

"Ohhh," I whined. "What about the anti-like potion? We didn't really give that a fair shot."

She tossed a wet paper towel at me. "You can't

keep running away from him. He lives next door to you! What are you going to do, sneak off to school early every morning for the rest of your life?"

"I guess not." I was tired of getting up extra early, anyway.

"I miss him," Phoebe said. "I miss him as a friend. I miss the three of us hanging out together, joking around, making up funny songs . . . and I bet you do, too. Talk to him. Set this straight. Clear the air. Then at least we might have a *chance* of having a good time at the skating party tomorrow."

Good old Phoebe. Even in matters of the heart, she's down-to-earth and practical. And in this case, I knew she was right.

"Okay," I said. "I'll talk to him as soon as I see him."

"Tonight?"

"If I see him tonight, then tonight," I said. "I can't talk to him if I don't see him."

"Tomorrow morning at the latest," Phoebe said. She can be tough when she wants to be.

"Tomorrow morning, do or die," I said, tipping my pirate hat to her.

"Aye, matey."

I walked home after school and went straight to my room. I couldn't wait to take off my pirate costume. No sign of Sam, not on the way home, or in his yard. To be honest, I was relieved that I was going to talk to him. I knew Phoebe was right, I had to come clean. It was just that as long as things were muddled, he was still my friend. He didn't hate me — yet. After I had my "talk" with him, I wasn't sure what would happen. But I knew he might get mad. He might be sad that I wasn't in love with him — and he might be angry that I handled this whole thing so badly, giving him the cold shoulder and avoiding him all week. He might even yell at me. I hate that, getting yelled at when I deserve it.

But getting yelled at would be better than the other possibility. I didn't know what would happen. But I was terrified it would be the end of our friendship.

Spirit Week, Day 5

Friday: Backwards Day

CHAPTER ELEVEN

COMING CLEAN

T-shirt: backwards. Check.

Denim mini: turned around so fly is in the back. Check.

Cardigan sweater: pre-buttoned and slipped over the head (too hard to button backwards when wearing). Check.

University of Maryland baseball cap: backwards. Check.

Heart locket: heart hanging down back. Check.

Somehow it felt right that Friday was Backwards Day. Everything in my life seemed turned around, headed in the wrong direction. Spirit Week was supposed to be fun, but this year it had been a complete disaster. Where did I go wrong?

All I could do was try to make the best of what

was left of the week. One last day. If I could just get things back to normal between me and Sam and Phoebe, I'd be happy.

Okay — happy-ish.

Satisfied.

Well, not too miserable. Spirit Week hadn't been as thrilling as I'd hoped. I guess there was always next year.

I laced up my pink sneakers. How do you wear shoes backwards? If I could turn my feet around, I would — that's how committed I was to Spirit Week, in spite of all that had happened. But I figured shoes were exempt from Backwards Day.

Mom helped me put my coat on backwards, zipping it up for me. "Have fun today, honey," she said. "Don't forget — tonight we're having Friday Night Surprise!"

Friday Night Surprise, which we have every Friday night so it's not *exactly* a surprise, is shrimp tacos. "How could I forget?" I said.

"Have fun at the skating party," she said.

I opened the front door and stepped outside.

There he stood, waiting for me. Sam Arkin. Friend, neighbor, carnation-giver, collage-maker. Unrequited liker.

I had to admit, he looked cute in his backwards

corduroy coat, backwards jeans, and a ski cap that might have been backwards but it was hard to tell because ski caps don't have obvious fronts and backs. Poor Sam. I imagined his big heart beating underneath the corduroy, still unbroken. Beating for me. If only he knew what was about to happen to it. I, Annabel Lawson, Sam's big crush, was about to crush him.

Snap out of it, Annabel. My romantic mind was getting carried away. But I couldn't help it. This was a sad day.

I took a deep breath. Time to break some hearts.

"Sam," I said. "I have to talk to you."

He laughed. "*You* have to talk to *me*! I've been trying to talk to you all week! But you keep acting weird and running away from me. What do you think, I have cooties or something?"

"Of course not," I said. We started walking to school.

"Then WHAT is your problem?" he said. "All I wanted to ask you is what Phoebe said about the red carnation."

What *Phoebe* said about it? That was a strange way to bring it up. I wasn't sure how to answer him. I knew what he wanted to hear: that Phoebe was

115

thrilled for us. That she loved the idea of me and Sam as a couple. That she couldn't wait to be maid-of-honor at our wedding.

But of course, that wasn't even close to true.

I tried to buy some time. "About the carnation," I said. "What did you mean by it, exactly?"

Sam crumpled his eyebrows in confusion. "What do you mean, what did I mean? Isn't the Flower Code clear? Pink stands for friendship, red stands for . . . you know." He blushed. He didn't want to say the word "crush." "Wait a minute. Do you mean Phoebe didn't understand what I meant? The way you were avoiding me, I was beginning to think she didn't like me at all."

"Of course she likes you," I said. "But we were both kind of stunned when I got a red carnation from you. I mean, *I* had no idea, *she* had no idea . . . we had no warning. It was just . . . there. A big fat red carnation, taped to my locker."

Sam's mouth fell open. "Say that again?"

"Say what again? Big, fat, red —"

"Taped to *whose* locker?" Sam said. "*Who* got a red carnation from me?"

"Um . . . *I* did." Did he have amnesia all of a sudden?

"But — I didn't send you a red carnation," Sam said. "I sent you a pink one."

"A what?" I said.

Now he looked worried — as if he was afraid he'd hurt *my* feelings.

"I sent you a *pink* carnation," he said slowly. "And a red one to Phoebe."

I stopped dead in my tracks. I felt dizzy. I tried to steady myself with a deep breath, but it wasn't working.

"Annabel? Are you okay?"

"But — I got the red carnation," I said. "And Phoebe got the pink one. We thought —"

I began to understand. Some cheerleader delivery girl must have mixed things up and delivered the carnations wrong.

"You thought — ?" His eyebrows crunched again. "Oh. Oh, no."

I started to laugh. "Yes. Oh, yes."

"You thought I liked you?" Sam said. "Like — like *that*? Red-carnation liked you?" He started laughing, too. "Is *that* why you've been avoiding me?"

I nodded. I couldn't talk because I was laughing so hard.

Ah. Good old Sam. Nice to have him back.

"Wait," I said when I could talk again. "So — you like Phoebe?"

"Yeah," he said. "You're not upset, right?"

"Of course not!" I said. "I'm relieved! I mean, I like you — as a *friend,* but . . ."

"And I like *you* as a friend," he said. "But you sure haven't been acting like a friend lately."

"I'm sorry about that," I said. "After I got that red carnation I was afraid you had a crush on me. And I was *really* afraid you were going to ask me to the skating party, especially after Phoebe told me —" I stopped. Would Phoebe mind if I told Sam she liked him, too? Or was it a secret?

Sam's face went white. "After Phoebe told you what?"

I couldn't do it. I couldn't betray Phoebe's confidence. I knew she liked Sam but I wasn't sure she wanted him to hear it from me.

"Let's just say this," I said. "Why don't you try telling Phoebe you like her again? Only this time, say it as clearly as you can. With words, not flowers."

"I tried to tell her four days ago," Sam said. "If only you would have talked to me!"

"I'm sorry," I said. "It's all my fault. I ruined Spirit Week!"

"Oh, Annabel," Sam said, laughing. "It's not your fault."

I felt a little better. "I'm still sorry for the misunderstanding."

"I'll make up for it today," Sam said. "I'm going to tell Phoebe I like her at the skating party. Just promise you won't say anything. I want to tell her myself. I want to surprise her."

"I won't say anything," I said. "But hurry up. I won't be able to keep this secret for long."

We arrived at school. Phoebe wasn't waiting for me on the steps, which was lucky because she would have suspected something if she saw me and Sam talking to each other again.

Sam and I went inside. A strange-looking boy moved awkwardly toward us down the hall. There was something very odd about the way he was walking. His feet were pointed in the wrong direction and he was wearing a monkey mask on his face.

"Hello," the monkey boy said. His voice seemed to come from the back of his head. Then he turned around. "Gotcha!"

I jumped. It was Charlie Mason, dressed backwards with a mask over the back of his head. He'd been walking backwards to confuse us. As I looked around the hall I got a funny dizzy feeling — all around me people seemed to be walking backwards. But they were actually walking forwards — it was just their clothes that were backwards.

"This is freaky," I said.

"Do you know how to ice-skate backwards?" Charlie asked. "I'm going to blow everyone's mind."

I laughed. "Try not to blow my mind while I'm on the ice. I have enough trouble staying upright as it is."

"Skating backwards isn't that hard," Charlie said. "Maybe I can teach you."

"Okay," I said. Was that an *indirecta*? The warning bell rang. "See you at the party."

Charlie left. "Did he just ask me out?" I asked Sam.

Sam shrugged. "Hard to say, Maybe he's just really into backwards skating." He started for his locker. "Remember — don't tell Phoebe my surprise."

"I won't, I won't," I said. I went to my locker. Phoebe wasn't there. I opened my locker — and there it was. Another note.

This time the collage was made of silver, white, and pale blue pictures — icy colors — pasted into a circle. It looked like a frozen pond or an ice rink. Inside, the note said, "See you at the skating party. — S.A." Why would Sam send me notes if he didn't have a crush on me?

I took the note and ran down the hall to Sam's locker. "Sam!"

Sam read the note. "Weird. What is this?" he said.

"I thought it was from you. It's signed with your initials," I said. "S.A. I've been getting these notes all week."

He laughed. "This S.A. doesn't stand for Sam Arkin — unless someone is trying to impersonate me."

"Then who is S.A.?" I ran through the names of all the boys in school, but I couldn't think of anyone else with those initials.

"Duh, Annabel," Sam said. "Did you ever consider that S.A. could stand for Secret Admirer?"

Oh my gosh. Secret Admirer!

"Who do you think it is?" Sam said.

"I have no idea," I said, feeling dizzy again. I'd had a secret admirer all week long and didn't realize it! I looked at the boys milling around me in their backwards baseball caps and backwards V-neck sweaters. Could it be Charlie? Oliver? Serge? Or Ari and Claire playing a mean joke?

"Well, I guess you'll find out soon enough." Sam tapped the note. "He said he'll see you at the skating party. Maybe he'll reveal his secret identity there!"

"I wish the party would hurry up and happen

already," I said. "I can't stand the suspense! I've got to find Phoebe and tell her!"

Sam grabbed my arm to stop me. "You can't do that," he said. "If you tell her I'm not S.A., then she might know I don't like you, and it could spoil my surprise! Please don't say anything to her, Annabel. The skating party's only a few hours away. Can't you just wait a few more hours?"

"Okay," I said. "But you owe me." I felt as bubbly as a bottle of anti-like potion — like I was ready to explode with excitement! *I* had a secret admirer!

First I had to get through half a day of school. To put it mildly, it dragged.

Spanish was okay because Señora Gomez let us have a Spirit Week Fiesta, so all we did was eat tortillas and sing Spanish songs while she played the guitar. That was fun.

Sitting through algebra was like listening to fingernails scratch on a chalkboard for forty-five minutes straight. Luckily, I wasn't the only one who couldn't concentrate. Almost everyone Mr. Mackey called on just stared at him slack-jawed.

I glanced at the clock on the wall. It was 10:30. An hour and a half to go. *Tick, tick, tick . . .*

In English class Ms. Yancy sent us to work on research papers in the library.

I settled in the periodical area, where the librarian had set up comfortable chairs around a big, low table covered with the latest magazines. Ari and Claire nabbed two of the other chairs and snatched up copies of *CosmoGirl!* and *Teen Vogue*.

I picked up my book and held it in front of my face so the librarian wouldn't see my mouth moving and know I was talking. That's the standard library technique.

"Hey, Ari," I whispered. "What did you finally tell Serge? Are you going to the skating party with him?" It was none of my business, but I was curious to know.

"She turned him down," Claire said. "So then he asked me."

"Claire, shut up," Ari said. "I mean, this is the library. We're not supposed to be talking."

Claire rolled her eyes at Ari.

The three of us sat quietly for a few minutes, turning pages. But none of us was reading. I could feel the tension in the air. Claire wanted to tell me the rest of the story, and I wanted to hear it.

Claire dropped her magazine. "So I turned Serge

down," she said. "I wanted to say yes but Ari told me I had to say no."

"I did not," Ari said. "Claire, you have total free will. You're responsible for your own actions. I only *suggested* that you could do better than Serge. We both could."

"So who are you going with?" I asked.

Silence. They both hid behind their magazines again.

Ari broke the silence first. "You know, seventh-grade boys are *really* immature. They're way too young for us."

"Yeah," Claire said. "From now on, Ari and I won't even *look* at a boy unless he's in eighth grade."

"That's our policy," Ari said.

"Everyone knows that girls mature faster," Claire said.

"Seventh-grade boys might as well be in kinder-garten," Ari said. "They're like babies."

"Totally," Claire said.

"What about Oliver?" I said. "I thought you liked him, Ari."

"She asked him to the skating party, but he said no!" Claire whispered.

"That's not true!" Ari said. "He said he was busy."

"He said he's going with someone else," Claire said.

"Who?" I said.

"We don't know," Claire said.

Could Oliver have said no to Ari because he was planning on ice-skating with *me*? Was he my secret admirer?

"Are you going to the skating party with a boy?" Claire asked.

I shook my head. "Not really."

"What does that mean?" Ari said.

"It means no," I said. I wasn't *going* to the party with a boy; I was meeting him there.

"You like someone," Claire said. "Is it Charlie?"

"What? No," I said. "I mean, I don't think so —"

"What do you mean, you don't think so?" Ari said. "Either you like him or you don't."

How could I explain? I might like Charlie if he was my secret admirer, but I didn't know yet.

"Do you like Oliver?" Ari asked.

"Um, about the same as Charlie," I said.

"Well you must like somebody," Ari said.

"Why?" I said.

"Because," Ari said.

"Come on, Annabel," Claire said. "You can tell us."

"Sorry," I said, turning back to my book. "I'm afraid that's top secret."

CHAPTER TWELVE

A BACKWARDS-DAY

MIRACLE

That Friday morning set a new record for endless-ness. But at last the noon bell rang and it was almost time for the highlight of Spirit Week: the Seventh Grade Ice-Skating Party. Most of all, it was almost time for me to find out who my secret admirer was.

But first: the Spirit Week Final Ceremony and Winchester Pirates Pep Rally.

The whole school gathered in the big main lobby, where the Spirit Week score chart was posted. The final scores had not been filled in yet. As of Thursday, the seventh grade trailed the eighth grade by only five points. The sixth-graders weren't even in the running.

The cheerleaders led us all in a round of our

school fight song, "Pirate Power." The halls were still echoing our cry of the last line, "We're brave and daring, we fight like heck, we'll make your team swab our deck," when Ms. Tabor stood up to announce the final scores.

"We'll never catch the eighth-graders," Phoebe said. "We've been running behind them all week."

"But every day we narrowed the gap," I reminded her.

"The final scores for this year's Winchester School Spirit Week are as follows," Ms. Tabor said. Mr. Dubrow stood on a ladder to write the final scores on the chart. "The sixth grade has 110 points. Good job, sixth-graders!"

The sixth-graders cheered. "Poor little things," Phoebe said. "They can't possibly think they're getting a pizza party, can they?"

"Maybe they're just filled with school spirit," I said.

"The seventh grade, after an excellent rally at yesterday's Pirate Festival and today's Backwards Day, finishes with 150 points!" Ms. Tabor announced.

Ms. Tabor paused and there was a loud cheer from the seventh graders.

"A hundred and fifty!" Phoebe said. "How did we do that?"

"Who cares?" I said. "That is a great score."

"Finally, the eighth grade comes in with a total of 145 points," Ms. Tabor said. "The seventh grade wins!"

The room erupted in cheers and boos. Phoebe and I jumped up and down. We hugged each other. We hugged Claire and Ari and Oliver and Charlie and Serge. We hugged every seventh-grader we saw.

"Congratulations, seventh-graders!" Ms. Tabor said. "Your Monday afternoon classes are canceled for a fabulous Pirate Pizza Party!"

We all cheered again. The eighth-graders stomped their feet and booed.

"Pizza party! All right!" Charlie said.

"I wonder how we pulled that off," Phoebe said.

"It's an amazing upset," I agreed.

"I heard a rumor that someone in our class pulled a Backwards-Day miracle," Oliver said.

"What kind of miracle?" I said.

"I'm not sure," Oliver said. "All I know is someone in our class nabbed a lot of bonus points today."

"Who? How?" Phoebe asked.

Oliver shrugged. "Maybe we'll find out at the skating party." He got a funny look on his face, and I thought about my secret admirer.

"All right, pirates!" Ms. Tabor shouted over the

noise. "Line up by class for your Spirit Week field trips. Eighth-graders, wait by the gym for your buses to the bowling alley. Sixth-graders, line up outside the auditorium for your trip to Gameland. And victorious seventh-graders, your buses to the ice rink will meet you right out front. Have a great time, everyone, and congratulations on another fantastic Spirit Week!"

"I can't believe it's over already," Phoebe said.

"Not quite yet," I said. "The best part's still to come."

Phoebe sighed. "Yeah, I guess ice-skating will be fun. Even if the week didn't go quite as we planned."

I had to pinch my lips together to keep from saying anything. If only she knew! In half an hour Sam would tell her he liked her, and I would find out the identity of my secret admirer, who — praise pirates — wasn't Sam.

We boarded one of the buses and rode to the rink, eating our bag lunches on the way. Phoebe sat next to me, but I couldn't say a word to her about Sam or my secret admirer, and since those two exciting secrets crowded out everything else in my brain, I didn't talk much.

"Are you mad at me?" Phoebe asked.

"No," I said. I tried to flash her a reassuring grin, but she didn't buy it.

"Did you talk to Sam yet?" she asked.

"Yes," I said.

"Well," she said. "What did he say?"

I was dying to tell her. But I couldn't.

"He was pretty cool about the whole thing," I said. "It went better than I thought."

"Good."

"Are you sure?"

"Positive."

She squinted her skeptical squint and settled back in her seat. "Something's up," she said. "I can feel it."

"Nothing's up," I said. "I'm just so excited about the skating party that I can hardly talk."

She squinted again, extra hard. "That doesn't sound like you at all, Annabel Lawson. Usually when you're excited about something you can't shut up about it."

"Maybe I'm changing," I said. "Getting mature, growing up."

"Growing up? Please. The only thing that can stop you from talking is a mouthful of peanut butter. Or a secret."

And that was true for sure. This year Spirit

Week had been all about secrets. Phoebe's secret crush on Sam. Sam's secret crush on me — or so I had thought. Then Sam's secret crush on Phoebe. And my secret admirer's secret identity.

"I'll get it out of you by the end of the day," Phoebe said.

I pursed my lips, desperately straining to keep my mouth shut. She was right — she *would* find out by the end of the day. But not from me, if I had an ounce of self-control left in my body. But I was down to maybe an ounce *at the most.*

I was so happy for Phoebe. The boy she liked liked her! I hoped I'd be just as happy when I found out who my own admirer was.

When we got to the ice rink we poured off the bus and rented skates. Phoebe and I wobbled onto the ice, trying to stay out of the way of the better skaters whizzing past.

"It takes me a few minutes to get my skating legs up to speed," Phoebe said.

Sam skated up to us and skidded to a stop. "Hello, girls," he said.

"Hi, Sam," I said.

"Hi, Sam," Phoebe said.

Sam offered Phoebe his mittened hand. "Would you like to skate with me a while, Phoebs?"

Her eyes got wide. She looked at me again, then back at Sam. Then she giggled nervously.

"Sure," she said. "I'd like that."

"Good," Sam said. "Because I've got some explaining to do." Sam kept talking. "I just found out I owe you a red carnation."

"What?" Phoebe took his hand and the two of them skated away. Phoebe glanced back at me with a big happy grin.

One mystery solved. One to go. I skated slowly around the rink, looking at all the boys, wondering when my secret admirer would appear and how he would reveal himself.

Charlie skated up to me, backwards, showing off. My heart beat faster. But he didn't stop, just glided past with a friendly wave. Then he spun around Claire, startling her and making her fall. "Claire! I'm sorry," he said. He offered his hand to help her up. I kind of got the feeling he'd knocked her down on purpose. It gave him a chance to bug her and hold hands with her at the same time.

So Charlie wasn't The One. And to tell the truth, I was glad. I liked him well enough but he didn't give me goose bumps or butterflies or dizziness or any of the other things you get when you really like someone.

Boy after boy skated by, some gracefully, some sloppily, one or two barely able to stay on their feet. Oliver Goodrow took both my hands and spun me around. *Oh my gosh,* I thought. But he let me go and moved on, spinning Ari, then Claire. He was going from girl to girl, spinning them around, trying to make them dizzy. Not a great quality in a boyfriend. If he has to literally spin you to make you dizzy for him, it isn't the real thing.

So who could S.A. be? I looked all around, left, right, in front, behind . . . *thump!*

I crashed right into someone and we both tumbled to the ice.

I took a minute to get my bearings. Sitting beside me was Alex, with all his clothes on backwards.

"Oh!" I cried. "I'm sorry. Your clothes threw me off. I thought you were going when you were coming."

"Yako s'taht."

"What did you say?" I said.

It was the first time I'd seen him that day. Not only was he wearing his clothes backwards, he'd even combed his hair backwards. He was actually participating in a Spirit Week activity.

"Hey," I said. "You're like Super Backwards Man. I thought you didn't do Spirit Week."

"Sknaht."

"What?" Why was he talking so funny? Had he hit his head when we fell?

"That's 'Thanks' in backwards talk," he said.

"How can anyone understand you if you talk backwards?" I said.

"They can't," he said. "It's a problem. I'll stop doing it now."

"Spirit Week is over," I said. "We won!"

"I know," Alex said. "No classes Monday afternoon. And I was supposed to have an algebra quiz."

Serge skated by and patted Alex's shoulder. "Hey, it's the hero of the day!" he said.

"Hero?" I said. "What did you do?"

"Nothing much," Alex said.

"Nothing much!" Serge said. "He wrote his English report backwards — and read it out loud in class! Backwards, of course. We couldn't understand a word, but Ms. Tabor said the backwards report scored us major bonus points. It was just enough to tip us over the edge and win the pizza party!"

"So *you're* the Backwards-Day miracle?" I cried.

"That's him!" Serge slapped Alex on the shoulder again and skated away. Alex blushed.

"I'm surprised," I said. "I thought you didn't like Spirit Week. I thought you didn't like going along with the crowd."

Alex shrugged. "I like Backwards Day," he said.

I laughed. "I'll say."

"Here," he said. "Let me help you up." He stood, then offered me his hand. I struggled to my feet.

"Um," he said. "Feel like skating around?"

I felt my cheeks get hot. "Okay," I said. Were those goose bumps rising on my arms?

We skated awkwardly around the rink. Neither one of us was too sure on our skates. Alex didn't hold my hand or anything. But still I could feel something in the air between us — something I'd never noticed before. I pushed up my sweater sleeve. The fine hair on my forearm was standing straight up, as if I'd rubbed my skin with a balloon. Yup. I definitely had goose bumps.

That's funny, I thought.

Alex skated to the side of the rink and held onto the wall. "Why are you stopping?" I said.

"Because I have to say something," Alex said. "And I can't talk and skate at the same time. Not very well, anyway."

"Oh," I said. "What is it?"

He looked down at his feet and mumbled something. It sounded like "Uoy ekil I."

"What? I couldn't understand you."

"Uoy ekil I." Now he was staring at the sky but said it a little louder this time.

"Uoy ekil I?" Was he speaking backwards to me again?

Uoy ekil I . . .

"I like you?" I said.

"You do?" Alex grinned, finally looking right at me.

"No, I mean, is that what you were trying to say?"

He nodded.

"So —" Suddenly the truth dawned on me. "Wait — are you my secret admirer?"

He nodded again.

Alex Hoffman was my secret admirer! I couldn't have been more shocked if he'd told me he'd just been elected president of Bolivia. My skates slipped out from under me, but I grabbed the wall before I fell again. For the second time that day I was blown away by a surprise. Mom wouldn't have to bother with the shrimp tacos after all.

"You made me those notes?" I said. I still couldn't quite believe it.

"Yeah," he said. "Dorky, I know."

"No! I liked them. They were great," I said. "But I had no idea they were from you." I looked at him again.

"Do you mind?" he said. "I mean, that I sent you those cards and everything?"

"No," I said. "I'm glad you did. I'm just surprised.

136

I never suspected it was you. I thought you hated Valentine's Day and all that . . . stuff."

"I never really liked Valentine's Day, it's true," he said. "All those hearts and things, pink and red, just because the calendar says it's February 14th. But when you like someone, you kind of want to let them know, even though you're kind of scared."

"I totally know what you mean," I said. "Because what if they don't like you back, right?"

"Right," Alex said.

He took my hand, mitten to mitten. I felt something fluttering in my stomach. My head began to spin, and my skin prickled. Goose bumps! Stomach butterflies! Dizziness! I had it all.

Oh my gosh! I thought. *I like Alex Hoffman!* I got more goose bumps just thinking his name.

And Alex liked me! It was the best February 18th ever, better than any February 14th I'd ever had.

"Well," I said, looking at my skates, "I like you, too."

"You do?" Alex asked. "Want to skate again?"

I looked him in the eye and nodded.

His face broke into a big smile.

I smiled back at him. "Okay."

We skated past Sam and Phoebe, hand in hand. I waved to them with my free hand and smiled.

Phoebe smiled and gave me a thumbs-up. Sam grinned. They looked adorable together. Phoebe and Sam. Me and Alex. It was a happy ending for everyone.

In spite of all the obstacles, misunderstandings, mix-ups, backwardness, and general insanity, it turned out to be a great Spirit Week after all. Who knew things were going to work out so well? And I had a feeling next year would be even more pirate-tastic! Yo ho ho!

"Victory!" Kaitlyn Sweeney declared. She strode up to the table in the Marshfield Lake Middle School cafeteria, the fingers of her left hand raised over her head in a *V*.

Her best friends, Liesel and Maggie, looked up from their lunches. Liesel flipped her shaggy blond bangs out of her eyes. "What victory?" she asked.

"I got the last brownie." Kaitlyn held up a walnut-studded square wrapped in plastic.

"Ew, nuts," Liesel said, wrinkling her nose.

Kaitlyn dropped her lunch tray on the table and slid into the seat across from Liesel. "I saw this guy looking at it, so I pretended I was just reaching for a milk. Then, at the last second, I snagged it from right under his nose."

Maggie rolled her eyes. "Kaitlyn, only you could turn buying a brownie into a competitive sport."

"Hey, you snooze, you lose." Kaitlyn unwrapped the brownie. "Anybody want a bite?"

Liesel shook her head. "Walnuts are vile." She'd always been a picky eater. For as long as Kaitlyn had known her — which was pretty much their whole lives — she'd lived mainly on grilled cheese sandwiches and root beer.

"Your loss," Kaitlyn said with a shrug.

"I'll take some," said Maggie, reaching for the brownie.

"Hey, I said a *bite*!"

"Vat wuff a bide," Maggie mumbled through a mouthful.

Maggie was the opposite of Liesel — she ate anything. While Liesel was small, Maggie was tall. She had long black hair that she wore in a braid down her back. Maggie played volleyball and ran on the track and cross-country teams. She had practice every day, and as a result she was *always* hungry.

Kaitlyn was right in between her friends: medium size, medium height, medium-length medium-brown hair. She sometimes joked that the three of them were the perfect set — they came with one in every size.

Kaitlyn polished off the rest of her brownie,

then started on a turkey sandwich. Liesel was halfheartedly nibbling at a plate of french fries, and Maggie was working on her second slice of pizza. As she chewed, Kaitlyn glanced around the cafeteria. The sounds of kids' voices bounced off the walls, and the room seemed charged with energy. *Maybe because it's Friday,* Kaitlyn thought. Everyone was excited about the coming weekend.

"Do you guys want to sleep over tomorrow night?" Liesel asked her friends. "My mom has a faculty party at the college, so she won't be home until late. She said we can order pizza."

"I'm in," said Maggie.

"I can't," said Kaitlyn. "I'm babysitting."

"Again?" Liesel heaved an exaggerated sigh.

Kaitlyn looked at her. "What?"

"It's just, you're *always* babysitting lately," Liesel said. "You babysat last Friday *and* last Saturday and the Saturday before that and the Saturday before *that*."

Kaitlyn couldn't deny it. Just six months before, at the beginning of seventh grade, she'd started babysitting for a few of her mom's friends. Word got out, and suddenly Kaitlyn had more babysitting jobs than she could keep up with.

Before she could say anything else, Maggie started to wave to someone across the room. "Hey, Nola!" she shouted.

"Who's Nola?" asked Kaitlyn. She turned to follow Maggie's gaze. A girl with long brown hair was standing at the edge of the cafeteria, holding a lunch tray and looking around uncertainly. She seemed relieved to see Maggie.

"Hi, Maggie," she said as she approached their table.

Maggie invited her to sit down. "These are my friends Kaitlyn and Liesel," she said.

Kaitlyn and Liesel both said hello.

"Nola's in my English class. She just moved here," Maggie added, unnecessarily. Kaitlyn could tell just by looking at her that Nola wasn't from Marshfield Lake. She was wearing a sweater vest over a crisp white shirt and pants with a crease that could have cut through butter. Her hair looked like she had spent a long time blow-drying it. Most kids at Marshfield Lake just wore jeans and T-shirts, and even the kids who spent a lot of time on their hair looked like they didn't.

"She's from California," Maggie added.

"Los Angeles," Nola said quickly, as if she didn't want to be mistaken for someone from some *other* part of California.

"Really?" Liesel perked up. "I've always wanted to go to L.A. I think it would be totally inspiring."

"Liesel's an artist," Maggie explained to Nola. "She's the best in the school."

Liesel shrugged. "I paint. It's no big deal."

"She's just being modest," Maggie told Nola. "Liesel's, like, a genius. She's going to be in this youth art show at the city museum next month. Only three middle schoolers in the whole district were invited. Everyone else is in high school."

"I went to that museum when we moved here," Nola said. "It's nothing like what we have in L.A. I think MOCA is really the best."

"I love mocha, too!" Maggie enthused. "Though my mom says I shouldn't drink coffee because it stunts your growth."

Nola gave her a contemptuous smile. "MOCA stands for Museum of Contemporary Art."

"Oh." Maggie blushed.

Kaitlyn frowned. Why did Nola have to say it like that? Maggie had only been trying to be nice.

"My class went to an Andy Warhol exhibit there," Nola went on. "He was this really famous artist from the sixties," she added, looking at Liesel.

"I *know* who Andy Warhol is," Liesel snapped. She glanced across the table at Kaitlyn with a look that said, *Who does this girl think she is?*

Kaitlyn gave a miniscule shrug in reply.

"Anyway," Maggie said quickly, "Kaitlyn is an amazing babysitter. You should see her at the elementary school. She's practically a celebrity over there."

"Yeah." Kaitlyn laughed. "The Wiggles have got nothing on me."

To Kaitlyn's surprise, Nola's face lit up. "Really? I babysit, too!"

From: AllieOop@cablewest.com
To: Hays3@amerimail.com
Sent: Saturday, July 21, 2007 5:54 PM
Subject: MISS YOU!
Attach: BEST FRIENDS 101.jpg

Hey, Mandy girl! Just got home and I am SO sad! :-(
I miss camp SO much! :,(Don't you?! I wish it could
last forever — real life is so boring! Or — as camp
counselor Bill-Take-A-Chill-Pill would say — "This is
not — I say NOT — acceptable!"
Of course, I know you're happy to be back with you-
know-who! Lucky dog! Please — you have to write
me back and tell me all about your big reunion!
YBFF (Your best friend forever!),
Allie

OBTW — I played our talent show DVD for my brother on the ride home, and guess what he said? Give up? "That girl who played those dudes in your skit was SO awesome!" You're such a star!

OBTW2 — Remember this picture?

Amanda laughed out loud as she scrolled down to a picture of her and another girl. They stood arm-in-arm, both wearing messy wigs and goofy, clown-like grins. She shook her head and was about to hit REPLY when Kate, her oldest friend, appeared in the doorway.

"Amanda!" Kate called out, running in with a wide grin on her freckled face. "I missed you so much! How was camp? You look so tan!"

Amanda jumped up and happily hugged her friend.

"You look tan, too!" she said, standing back after a moment. "I thought it rained a lot in Ireland."

"It *does*," said Kate. "Believe me! There was literally moss growing on my shoes." She smiled and turned her head from side to side. "This is from my sister's self-tanner. I snuck a little this morning. Not too orange?"

Amanda nodded her approval. "No, it's good. But you missed a spot, right there." She pointed to

Kate's neck and giggled as her friend quickly tucked in her chin.

"I'll have to get that later," said Kate. Then she laughed and grabbed Amanda's hand. "Right now, I want to hear all about camp. Oh!" She reached into her pocket. "But first, I brought you this!"

She pulled out a small green box and handed it to Amanda, who opened it at once. Inside was a silver ring with two hands holding a heart and a crown on top. It was one of the prettiest things Amanda had ever seen!

"It's a Claddagh ring," Kate told her. "I got it in the village where my grandma grew up. It *can* be a symbol of love," she explained, "with the hands and the heart and all. But lots of people wear them as friendship rings, too. Do you like it?"

"I love it!" said Amanda, slipping the ring on and admiring how it looked on her hand. "Thanks so much!"

"Wait," Kate told her, grinning. "You've got to wear it like this." She took the ring from Amanda's finger and turned it upside-down. "This way, heart out, means you're available; your heart is open." She worked her eyebrows up and down. "The other way, heart in, means someone's already captured your heart. And we don't want anyone thinking you're not available, now, do we?"

Amanda laughed — weakly. *If Kate only knew!* And that's when she almost, *almost* spilled her summer secret. But she couldn't.

Guess what, Kate? There are some people who think I'm unavailable. A whole camp *full of people, in fact! How crazy is that? What made them think that? Funny you should ask. Turns out, I lied and said I had a boyfriend. No, really. I did!*

Of course, Amanda hadn't *meant* to lie. It just kind of . . . happened.

"Okay!" said Kate, plopping down in Amanda's desk chair. "I'm ready. What was camp like? How were the counselors? Did you make any friends?"

Amanda took a deep breath and tried to think about where to begin.

Of course Kate would want to know everything about camp. After all, it had been her idea to go the summer arts camp in the first place! (Camp was a loose term, since it was held on the campus of a tiny all-girl college — without a single tent or cabin or canoe for miles around!) They signed up to go *together*, of course, like everything they'd done since first grade.

It was all planned out: Amanda would play her cello, and Kate would play her flute. By the end of camp, they'd both be good enough to make first chair in orchestra in the fall. Not the most exciting summer, Amanda thought, but way better than baby-sitting Kate's little brother and sister at the pool, like last year.

This perfect plan, however, was not meant to be. Instead of spending three carefree weeks rooming with Amanda and becoming an expert at playing her flute, Kate had been whisked off to Ireland with the rest of her family. Her grandmother was turning 75, and had decided the whole gang should help her celebrate in the tiny town where she was born.

And Amanda? Well, Amanda ended up making a million new friends, not touching her cello once, and having the absolute best summer ever (despite one massive, ridiculous, totally *accidental* lie).

This Isn't Just Babysitting, It's War!

Kaitlyn is the top babysitter in Marshfield Lake—until super-sitter Nola moves to town and starts stealing Kaitlyn's clients away. When the ultimate babysitting gig comes along, how far will Kaitlyn go to defend her turf?

Will Jenny survive middle school?

Jenny's happy to start school with her best friend, Addie, by her side. But Addie has other plans—and they don't include Jenny!

Addie's running for class president and there's only one way to stop her—Jenny will have to run against her.

The school gossip column is revealing everyone's secrets! Can Jenny figure out who the snitch is?

CANDYAPP6

SCHOLASTIC

www.scholastic.com

SCHOOLBLST